lso by Jim Miller

ith Mike Davis and Kelly Mayhew) *Under the Perfect Sun:*
e San Diego Tourists Never See (New York, 2003)

ith Kelly Mayhew) *Better to Reign in Hell: Inside the*
iders Fan Empire (New York, 2005)

.) *Sunshine/Noir: Writing from San Diego and Tijuana*
 Diego, 2005)

Drift

A

(w
Th

(w
Ra

(ed
(Sa

Drift

a novel
Jim Miller

To Lily
Best
Jim Miller

UNIVERSITY OF OKLAHOMA PRESS : *Norman*

Line drawings by Perry Vasquez, courtesy of the artist.

Photographs on pages 2, 114, 130, and 178 by Jennifer Cost, courtesy of the photographer. Visual art and photography also courtesy of San Diego City Works Press (www.cityworkspress.org).

Photographs on pages 40 and 52 © San Diego Historical Society, used with permission.

Miller, Jim, 1965–
  Drift : a novel / Jim Miller.
      p. cm.
   ISBN 0-8061-3807-6 (alk. paper)
   ISBN 978-0-8061-3807-7
   1. California, Southern—Fiction. I. Title.
PS3613.I5384D75 2007
813'.54—dc22

The paper in this book meets the guidelines for permanence and durability of the Committee on Production Guidelines for Book Longevity of the Council on Library Resources, Inc. ∞

1 2 3 4 5 6 7 8 9 10

To all the people, places, and moments lost but for memory

and

to Kelly for everything

Acknowledgments

I owe a special debt to Matt Bokovoy for believing in and guiding this project. Special thanks go to Ellen Berry for her insightful editorial advice and incredible generosity of spirit and to Mel Freilicher for his careful reading and thoughtful criticism. I am also grateful for the encouragement and intellectual fellowship of the following people who read and commented on this novel: Josh Baxt, Jennifer Cost, Mike Davis, Hector Martinez, Alys Masek, Kelly Mayhew, Perry Vasquez, and Donna Watson.

In a dérive one or more persons during a certain period drop
their usual motives for movement and action, their relations,
their work and leisure activities, and let themselves be drawn
by the attractions of the terrain and the encounters they
find there.

GUY DEBORD *Theory of the Dérive*

✦ ✦ ✦

And these tend inward to me, and I tend outward to them,
And such as it is to be one of these more or less I am,
And of these one and all I weave the song of myself.

WALT WHITMAN *Song of Myself*

✦ ✦ ✦

There is no document of civilization which is not at the same
time a document of barbarism.

WALTER BENJAMIN *Theses on the Philosophy of History*

Drift

the heart of the city beautiful

1   Joe took a sip of coffee, stared at the screen and wrote: *There are these moments I have which bring me to full life, but I can't hold them. I can't sustain the nakedness, the shattering question, the permanent impermanence, so I retreat to the old lies which I tell myself are newer and truer than the fleeting moments. Everything fades and memory recasts the story. Am I ever truly present, fingering the rough, wondrous grain of now? There is a longing, an insatiable hunger with emptiness at its core. How do you nurse the ecstasy of becoming? How do you not close yourself off? Do you want to see me? Forget the dull trance of the dead world and hold the first scent of bloom, dive into the accidental glimpse of the street lined with the impossible purple of jacarandas . . .*

He looked at the screen, shook his head, and erased what he had written. The phone rang. Joe let the machine get it.

"This message is for Mr. Joe Blake. My name is Tina from Citibank MasterCard. Please call me immediately at 419-555-7781 regarding your account."

Joe wondered if some generations of people lived richer lives than others. He walked over to the coffee table and sorted through his unopened mail, the ads for pizza, insurance, and dating services, and the envelope from South Bay College. His heart sank and he opened it:

Dear Mr. Blake:

The search committee has selected several finalists for the position of Assistant Professor of English at South Bay College.

I am sorry to inform you that you were not among those chosen for a second interview. The search committee and South Bay College would like to thank you for your interest. We would welcome your application for future positions.

Sincerely,
Professor Bob Blank
Search Committee Chair

He dropped the letter in the trash and walked back over to turn off the computer. At least that was the last rejection for the year. No more ass kissing or self-promotion for another ten months. Sometimes he wondered why he kept at it, teaching five classes at three different campuses, not making enough money to pay off his debts or move out of a studio. He loved the rare moments of connection and insight, but it really came down to hating everything else more. Sometimes Joe wondered if he even wanted a full-time position. Money and benefits were great but what about the tedious sameness? He thought about the sexless mediocrity of Professor Bob Blank and the earnest, pious faces of the search committee. He knew he'd blown the question on "quantitative measured outcomes." Whatever. At least with Joe's invisible downward mobility came a kind of freedom. He was anonymous; he didn't matter that much. This was better than driving an SUV, better than a cell phone, better than owning things that seduced you into numbness.

Joe began to feel lighter. He pulled on a shirt, grabbed his wallet and walked out of his studio. Something about the hallway was always a little film noir, full of inconsequential mysteries. As he opened the door, Joe saw a pair of black leather shoes disappear up the old wooden staircase. He turned and walked down the hallway, glancing at the intricate flower pattern on the fading red and black carpet—stylized, Modernist. A strange mixture of garlic, fresh laundry, and cigarette smoke was in the air and the dying man in number eight was listening to Italian opera on his stereo. The moans of a woman's pleasure spilled out of number seven and someone in number five was chanting an incomprehensible mantra. Joe looked up at the gorgeous, fake crystal light fixture midway toward the front door and passed by the mail boxes and the mirror beside the rickety elevator, quickly moving into the luminescent sunlight emerging out of the shadows of the hallway.

Out on Fifth Avenue, Joe blinked and squinted in the blinding glare. It was one of those late spring days when the sky is so blue and brilliant that it seems unreal. He walked past a row of jacarandas in full purple bloom, some ugly, indistinguishable new beige and terra cotta condos, a tan 1920s mission-style apartment complex with marble steps, a Polish restaurant, Captain Smith's Bail Bonds, the Imperial House, a white Spanish-style apartment building, and a gourmet restaurant that used to be a bank. When he hit Laurel Street, he turned right, passed a stately old Craftsman embellished with round stones, and crossed Sixth Avenue into Balboa Park. He was greeted by a huge Moreton Bay Fig and more rich purple jacarandas. The limbs of the big eucalyptus trees and Canary Island pines were gently swaying in the breeze as Joe made his way toward the Laurel Street Bridge. He stopped and glanced at the bronze statue of Kate Sessions, who had transformed this barren mesa into a stunning garden of borrowed flowers. Just over her stiff Victorian shoulder, Mexican boys turned tricks in the bushes and hapless tourists wandered by cruisers. Joe walked on, glancing over at the bright white outfits of the lawn bowlers playing amidst the pink apricot blooms and cherry blossoms. Further on, he watched a chihuahua chase a greyhound in "dog park". From the middle of the bridge, Joe looked down at Highway 163 cutting through the canyon, surging toward the downtown skyline and the Coronado Bridge beyond it. As he approached the main entrance to the park, the California Building rose above him, its ornate tower looming grandly, the cobalt blue and gold tiled dome glistening in the midday sun.

Joe was struck by the stark juxtaposition of Bertram Goodhue's Spanish Revival fantasy and the spare Administration Building that preceded it. The latter, built by Irving Gill, was an austere mission-style Craftsman box, ready to yield itself to the surrounding landscape, be covered by vines, honed and molded by the elements. The California Building announced an illusion of a romantic Spanish past that had never existed. It was a concrete manifestation of the desire for history without blood. Joe could almost see docile, humble Indians coming in for a mass led by a benevolent padre. It was a gorgeous delusion, a marvelously seductive lie.

In fact, this one intersection at the threshold of the park represented the outcome of the formative clash between the two factions of Anglo elites who reconstructed San Diego out of the stuff of their dreams after it was stolen from Mexicans and the indigenous peoples before them. George Marston and the Progressive Anglo oligarchy wanted Gill and the Olmsted brothers to build a garden city, pure and uncorrupted by the vulgar boosters, an ideal Mediterranean city on the Pacific where migrants from the East could come for health as well as spiritual and cultural renewal. It was to be the heart of the City Beautiful, where the poet's dream was realized in the form of meandering paths designed to surprise, delight, and inspire wonder in nature. On the other hand, John Spreckels, the son of a robber baron who built an empire in Hawaii, the owner of railroads, the *Union-Tribune*, the Hotel del Coronado, and prime downtown and waterfront real estate, wanted a marketable fantasy to promote the Panama California Exposition in 1915, and later streetcars, suburbs, profitable sprawl. For the boosters, the park was the pretty sister of commerce, not a utopian playground for vacillating dreamers. Spreckels won the battle, Gill and the Olmsteds quit, and garden culture was made to serve the interests of mammon. Joe had read the history but today he couldn't help but be seduced by the way the sun hit the grand old facades. For a moment they struck him the way they did when he first came to San Diego from Toledo, Ohio. Beautiful without irony.

As he walked through the main entrance to the park, Joe stopped for a moment and stared up at the elaborate friezes above the door of the California Building, the figures of Vancouver, Cabrillo, Serra and other conquerors, priests, and angels. He watched a series of tourists stop to take pictures. People went in and out of the Museum of Man. He looked down the Prado at the junk buildings, made to fall apart a few years after the Exposition. Millions of dollars had been spent to keep them standing for more than eighty years. With the Expositions of 1915 and 1935, the boosters had turned the park into a commodity that offered the crowd a few hours of emancipation. It was both cynically commercial and unintentionally utopian at the same time.

Joe stood and watched the stream of pedestrians drifting in and out of the park—a Somali woman in a dark blue robe, an old white man jogging in short shorts with no shirt on, two Mexican teenagers stopping to kiss under the arched entryway, a man with long dreds, headphones, and big mirrored shades, Japanese children hopping on the museum stairs. He glanced back up at the wings of an angel with the face of a newborn babe. The magic of the building was that it was anything you wanted it to be. Orson Welles had used it as Xanadu in *Citizen Kane*, the wondrous palace that housed a heart of darkness. But as Joe stared at the building, the inessential features melted away and he was left staring at something outside of history—an image of a past that had never existed. It was not something in a chronology, but a space in the imagination, a blank site for the play of fancy. Joe thought for a moment about the crowds that had strolled here in the teens and the thirties. What had been their troubles and joys? Did they imagine him here after their deaths as he thought of those who might be here later? The far end of the country had still been new for them. By the time Joe had come west, it had long since stopped being a frontier of any sort. Indeed, even the narratives of paradise lost were a cliché by now.

As he walked on, Joe caught a glimpse of the reproduction of the Elizabethan Old Globe Theatre through one of the arches that led out of the corridor of the California Building. He paused by the Modernist sculpture garden, changed course and crossed over to Alcazar garden, modeled on the one in Seville. Here he stopped and swam in color and light. The central flowerbeds were a riot of red, yellow, purple, pink, fuchsia, and white zinnias, petunias, and chrysanthemums. The sun was warm on his face and the air was full of floral perfume. Joe closed his eyes for a moment and listened to the water trickling in two small fountains, opened them again and lost himself in the redness of red impatiens, the blueness of a lily of the Nile. He tried to dig himself deeper into the heart of the moment, but it eluded him, sliding away coyly. Joe passed by a man on a bench with despair in his eyes, an old lady smelling a flower petal she had picked up off the ground, a bored bride posing for a picture, and a man with a video camera filming the blank wall of the House of Charm. He left the garden and strolled around to the front of the building past a big statue by Niki de Saint Phalle called "Poet and Muse," a child's dream in multicolored tile.

Joe crossed the parking lot, glancing over at a big fountain and the Spanish Colonial Museum of Art before walking through the corridor of the House of Hospitality to get to the Museum of Photographic Arts. *Sunset Boulevard* was showing in the theater. He paid for the film and wandered through the museum to kill some time before it started. The exhibition was a survey of pictures from the permanent collection, a little bit of everything. Joe glanced at a picture by Ansel Adams, Half Dome in Yosemite in black and white. Adams' photo was not nearly as beautiful as the rush of long, thick, black hair on the woman looking at a picture by Robert Frank. Her head was slightly tilted to the side, exposing her neck and a smooth brown shoulder. She was looking at a shot of a sad, dingy fifties diner, three lonely figures sipping coffee at the counter, not talking or looking at the camera. A sign on the wall behind them said "No Loitering. No Free Refills." As the woman turned to look at the next picture, Joe could smell her, deeply sweet. She had big, brown eyes, sharp features—serious, intelligent, Indian. She didn't smile or say anything. Joe liked that. He felt his body come alive and walked the other way to look at a photo of Paris in the 1920s. It was a picture of a prostitute smoking in an empty cafe. Her face was not over-made and her short dress did not fit well. In the shadows of the cafe she seemed to be deep in thought, almost praying. Joe moved on to a picture of the first moon walk, Dexter Gordon smoking and holding his sax, a Buddhist temple in the jungle at dawn in Thailand, an elephant in Africa, a dead man lying in a pool of blood, shot by a soldier for holding a sign. It was 2:00, time for the film.

The curator was finishing his introduction to the film as Joe made his way into the theater. He said something about Hollywood commenting on itself and the lights went down. Joe was immediately drawn into late forties black-and-white LA in decay. The mission-style, Spanish-style, Modernist, and Art Deco buildings were already relics of a broken dream. There's nothing to do in the gorgeous sunshine but rot while you tan. William Holden is a broke, cynical screenwriter from Ohio trying to stay one step ahead of the debt collectors and repo men. He plays at being the artist but knows it's too late. It's all a big scam in this town of false promises. Joe smiled self-effacingly at the notion that he was part of a long tradition of downwardly mobile white guys from the Midwest with artistic pretensions, bemoaning their fate, bemoaning the state of the culture. Holden's character falls into the surreal fantasy world of Gloria Swanson, a faded star whose butler, ex-husband, and ex-director, Erich Von Stroheim, helps maintain her grand delusions. Here Holden lives as a kind of pathetic gigolo, housed in the deteriorating mansion of the insane starlet, rewriting her ridiculous "comeback script" while she engages in a regimen of horrendous beauty treatments to bring back her youth. He gives up his life, his friends, his true love, and his writing for money, clothes, and a gilded cage. He watches her old movies with her and plays cards with Buster Keaton, Anna Q. Nilsson, and H. B. Warner. When he is finally overcome with self-revulsion and tries to break free, Swanson shoots him and turns her arrest into a grotesque final screening, preening for the cameras as they take her away. Appropriately, Holden dies and falls in the pool, an absurd corpse floating in the mad waters of obscene wealth.

After leaving the theater, Joe walked out into the late afternoon sun, pondering the fact that he lived in a state with such a rich tradition of self-promotion and disillusionment, dreams of Arcadia and apocalypse. As he made his way back out of the park, Joe thought about the rejection letter and another year of scraping by. When he had moved here for school, he knew he was never going back to Toledo, but he wasn't sure what he wanted to do. He still wasn't. Most of his friends from graduate school had moved on to doctoral programs or bigger cities. Those who remained he only saw occasionally at random parties. It didn't bother him much, though. He had little ambition and the weather was nice here. He'd escaped the daily dread and pain of family and the resigned desperation of the rust belt. San Diego was cheaper than San Francisco, more manageable than LA, a nice place to drift for a while. Unlike his old grad school friend Mike, a local boy who'd stayed in town and gotten a job working as an activist for the labor council, Joe wasn't rooted enough to fight the good fight. He didn't want to nurse his anger and play the role of Sisyphus in ultra-conservative "Bland Diego." People deserved a piece of the pie, but they didn't need that much, he thought. Maybe if he'd had kids, he'd feel differently. But he couldn't even imagine marriage, children, a house full of the ties that bind. Joe didn't have the bitterness of a film noir hero because he didn't believe in the dream. He longed for things he couldn't buy, things he couldn't even put into words.

Looking down at the highway under the bridge as he walked, Joe noted the hard, frenzied jazz of rush hour traffic, the red taillights angrily flashing. He rambled on, over the bridge, turned left, and went down the path toward Marston Point. Men were meeting up and talking in parked cars, sometimes driving off, other times not. A police car cruised by slowly, menacingly. Joe nodded to a sailor in a Mazda, crossed paths with a family of tourists with matching Disneyland shirts and Dallas Cowboys hats. A single blue heron flew overhead and the sunlight was filtering through the hanging limbs of the eucalyptus trees. At the vista point, Joe looked across the downtown skyline at the shimmering harbor, full of promise, with the deep blue Pacific just beyond it, out of sight. As he walked down the steps on the far side of the hill, he passed through an army of the dispossessed. Filthy and sunburned, they camped out here on blankets or plastic trash bags on the grass under the trees, taking refuge from the concrete city. It was a bloom of misery in the midst of the garden. Joe gave away all of his change to a woman who said she was hungry for God. She reeked of stale sweat and her face, once pretty, was now wrinkled and weather-beaten. But her eyes were beautiful, intense, burning with madness. "I could eat God," she told Joe, "and spit out fire on the city." He wondered how she'd gotten here, what her story was, and thought about what William Holden had said to sum up Gloria Swanson: "The dream she had clung to so desperately had enfolded her."

2   *The debate about where to place the main exposition site for the Panama-California affair was solved in 1911 when robber baron John D. Spreckels, the owner of the San Diego Electric Railway company, withheld his stock subscription pledges until a location was chosen that would please the street car and real estate interests, one conducive to running a rail line through the park and further increasing their property values to the North and East. Once the Exposition Company capitulated on this matter, Spreckels and the boosters went to work to make sure that the San Diego County Building Trades Council would not succeed in pressuring Mayor James Wadham and the City Park Commission into ensuring that more local union labor would be used in the building of the Exposition. The bankers and business interests represented by the Expo-*

sition's Board of Directors, on the other hand, wanted full control and cheap labor. Mayor Wadham, upon returning from a long drunk in San Francisco, gave in to the business interests and the entire City Park Commission resigned only to be replaced by members of the Exposition's Board of Directors.

With these victories under their belts, the boosters celebrated. At the ground breaking, they held a pontifical military mass on the future site of the Exposition that was followed by a grand fiesta that lasted half a week. On a sunny day in July, a liberal interpretation of a "Spanish caravel" sailed across the glistening harbor from North Island to the Broadway pier. There, "King Cabrillo" was carried up Broadway in a sedan chair by Anglos dressed as Indian peasants. At the courthouse, they stopped for the coronation of "Queen Ramona" (based on the character from Helen Hunt Jackson's sentimental novel Ramona, *the* Uncle Tom's Cabin *for California's Indians), who waited on her throne dressed in an Edwardian interpretation of Spanish Renaissance clothing. After the august ceremony, the royal couple then proceeded up Broadway to the carnival booths at "the Isthmus," followed by a throng of 10,000 people, not many of whom had read* Ramona. *Perhaps a number of them had been cheated out of union jobs by the boosters. But today, that didn't matter. Their future was a blue sky. They were part of something bigger.*

The "Historical Pageant," on the next day, included floats celebrating the conquering of the Aztecs by the Spanish and Mexico by the Americans. This was followed, on the final day, by "The Pageant of the Missions," which gave about a thousand locals a chance to dress up as Indians, Spanish imperialists, and Franciscan friars in the midst of historical facsimiles of the mythic mission past. Imperial San Diego was born and the San Diego Union-Tribune *declared: "The weaker was absorbed by the stronger; but with the passing of the weaker they left a legacy of their art and culture, which the survivor has gladly possessed to beautify and decorate his own. We have re-*

ceived this tradition gladly; we have made of this romance the back-ground of our own history in the fair port of San Diego and on the golden coast of California."

Actual Indians had lived in the park during the decades prior to its development. Local whites, however, were disturbed by the presence of what Harriet Goodbody called "big black savages." Miss Goodbody, whose family owned a farm near the park, noted that the Indians caused "quite a good deal of trouble by taking what did not belong to them." Despite these early conflicts, some Native Americans worked on the construction of the Exposition that displayed "things native" with imported "show Indians" from New Mexico in an exhibit called "The Painted Desert." Down the road in Mission Hills, signs were posted that read "Anglos Only."

3   Dying twilight trailed in through the door and was lost in the numb glow of the fluorescent lights in Room 113, where Joe's 7:00 P.M. English 101 class was meeting at Central College. The dim chattering subsided for a moment as he took roll, noting the absences, matching the names with the faces. Dewayne Foster in his security guard uniform, with his Denzel Washington looks and perfect posture; Maria Gonzales in her nurse's outfit, her sad, earnest face full of work and worry; Dan Griffith dressed to tend bar, slouching in his chair, nodding off under his down-turned Yankee's cap in the back row; Horace Johnson, not here; Rufus Larson, ambling in slowly in a black and silver Raiders jersey, red sweats, head phones buzzing, kind, sleepy eyes. Joe marked the roll book, remembered the way silence felt as a child. The smell of perfume in the room was battling with the odor of Ben Gay. Li Nguyen was reading a textbook, biting the end of his pen with a look of profound contemplation. Ernestine Peppers hobbled in slowly with her cane, dropping her large, fragile, elderly frame roughly into a seat by the door. Sofía Quintana sat next to her, bored and full of the easy beauty of youth. She had delicate features, dyed blond hair, a nose ring, and a pierced belly button that she never failed to reveal. There was a tattoo of barbed wire and roses around her left arm. Omar Ramiz and three others were absent. Theresa Sanchez smiled as Joe glanced at her, her eyes meeting his directly, as if with a question, in a way that made him feel totally exposed. Matt Thompson looked vaguely hostile in a business suit.

Joe felt the weight of the end of the semester—the accumulation of work, family, boredom, struggle, joy, failure, dread, anticipation, and tragedy was palpable. At the University of the Sun, his students were gearing up for expensive vacations and summer internships at corporate offices, but it was not like that here. These students were older, had worked and lived more. They didn't have much money, but they had more to lose and gain. Joe was glad that his only summer class would be here. Frank Villone nodded to him amiably. His hat was an ad for a brand of auto parts. Laila Washington's eyes were red from weeping, but her face told Joe not to ask. Sometimes these ugly old rooms were so full of pain, beauty, and raw being that Joe felt utterly humble. Jasmine Zamora was giggling at him and the quiet had vanished into a low rumble of dissonant talk.

"Okay," Joe said, hearing his own voice, strange, disembodied, "everybody please pass up your essays." The students unzipped backpacks, opened folders, and a stream of white paper came forward. Joe walked from row to row to collect them, put the stack on the front desk and started into the night's work. They corrected a few sentences on the board, reviewed a citation rule, and moved on to discuss their essays on their favorite poem.

"What did you find?" asked Joe.

"That poetry sucks," Sofía quipped glibly. There was a long, hard silence. Their eyes were fixed on their desktops or out the door at the inviting darkness. Joe smiled and waited.

"Is a song a poem?" asked Ernestine.

"Sure it is," said Joe.

"Then I found Billie Holiday," Ernestine continued. "The words ain't much, but she say it well."

"That's how poetry started," Joe said. "Anybody else?"

"Langston Hughes' poems sound like blues," said Dewayne. "I had to read some in another class. They real simple, easy to understand, but there's a lot of meaning in 'em."

"Like what?" asked Joe.

"Like about racism," answered Dewayne.

"Did you like them?" Joe pressed.

"They all right I guess," replied Dewayne with finality. Frank raised his hand politely and Joe called on him.

"Were we supposed to just find anything or something that we thought was important?" he asked.

"Something that meant something to you," Joe said.

"I found Neruda," interrupted Theresa, "a poem called 'A Dream of Trains.'"

"What did you like about it?"

"There was a line in it about being alone in a crowd of people who are alone too. It reminded me of walking down the street wondering about people. You know, who are they and what are they thinking? It seemed true. I think we all do that sometimes." She finished and looked at Joe with an expression of tacit understanding. He nodded and looked at her eyes, serious, alive, searching.

"Maybe that's what poetry is all about," said Joe, "finding moments of truth. Otherwise why would people do something so useless? Maybe poems give us something we can't get anywhere else. Meaning, connection. What do you think?" He stopped and noticed a single tear rolling down Laila's face. Dan was asleep. Sofía and Matt were rolling their eyes. Li raised his hand eagerly.

"Buddhist poems are about true moments. Like beauty in nature."

"Can we have a break?" interrupted Jasmine.

"Sure," Joe said. "Let's take fifteen minutes." He answered a few questions about late papers and walked out of the classroom, across the quad, toward the faculty restrooms. It was a clear night and the

17

downtown skyline stood out boldly in the immediate distance, the corporate towers and high rise condos announcing themselves as the new lords of the transformed city, with the surviving old buildings, petty traffic, and street life rustling below insignificantly. As Joe walked around the humanities building, he could see the lights on the Coronado bridge and in the windows of the funky old houses that lined the streets leading up to Golden Hill. There was nothing that suggested hope and human comfort to him more than a light in a window on a dark street. In the bathroom, he took a leak and wondered what had happened to his student, Bob Anderson, who told him he had lost his house last week and had nowhere to go. Joe had offered him money, but he refused, too proud. Joe washed his hands and looked in the mirror. There were dark circles under his tired green eyes. He looked pale and had forgotten to shave. For a second or two he felt utterly lost, unable to recognize the person staring back at him. He splashed some water on his face, ran his fingers through his thick brown hair, and headed back to the classroom to wrap up for the evening.

Later that night, back in his studio, Joe sipped a beer and glanced over a few of the essays he had collected. Frank Villone had found a horrible poem by Rod McKuen and ended his essay with the question, *"Why would anybody pay money to buy a book like this?"* Laila Washington had chosen Shakespeare's Sonnet 71 and had written: *"The speaker in this poem says 'No longer mourn for me when I am dead' and goes on to tell his lover to forget him if his memory brings sorrow to the lover. This sounds nice, but I think Shakespeare asks too much of a person. There are some memories that stay with you and won't go away. Maybe sorrow is God's way of showing us something. When my brother died of AIDS, he told me not to cry, but I couldn't stop and still can't when I think of him. It's too easy to say 'No longer mourn for me.' People can't do that."* Sofía Quintana wrote about "The Sick Rose," by William Blake: *"This poem is about how the heart of love is full of disease. The Rose is beautiful but sick with death inside of it. Depressing."*

Joe looked through the pile until he found Theresa Sanchez's essay about Neruda: *"Neruda's poems are about living a full life. He turns his dreams into beautiful words. After I read his poems, I see things more clearly—not differently, just more vividly. It's like he's trying to squeeze all the beauty out of the world and have it all at once. We are all 'alone in the loneliness,' trying to find our own truths. The world gets in the way, but if you try hard, you can see things more truly. All we have is this life and each other. I don't know if this makes sense, but that's how I see it."* At the bottom of the page, there was a handwritten note: *"Hey professor, I have to drop your class because of work, but I'd like to see you 'outside' of class."* Joe stared at the phone number at the bottom of the page and thought about the light in Theresa's eyes.

◆ *The city was once unnamed. Before the conquest, the Diegueño, Luiseño, Cupeño, and Cahuilla thought of themselves as part of the canyons, arroyos, and sea. Driven by the cycles of nature and the rhythms of the sun and moon, they did not know a way of being ruled by abstractions. Their concept of the holy was not polluted by an original sin. They were not at the center of their map of the world. When the priests and soldiers came and set up the Missions, they brought clock time to California. Originally invented in the Middle Ages as a way to honor God, the clock had become its own deity. The priests who ran the Spanish Missions used it to structure the day and push the indigenous peoples into a prison of measured time. Along with the workday, the padres also sought to impose Christian notions of sin and humility. But the original Californians knew no shame. One padre was actually castrated and killed by the Indians for his efforts to restrict the sexual practices of his flock. Of course, this battle was lost and the natives were taught time, work, and shame by the musket and lash. The city was named and the map of Christendom was enlarged.*

San Diego's first booster, Alonzo Horton, imagined a city larger than the small settlement at Old Town. He hired a surveyor and the Horton-Locking map that resulted in 1867 was a vision of a future city by the sea. He built a grand resort hotel, the Horton House, in the middle of nowhere and hoped people would come. His luck could not have been better than when Helen Hunt Jackson came with Abbott Kinney as Special Commissioners of Indian Affairs to tour San Diego County. Shortly after, Miss Jackson dreamed Ramona *and gave Horton a golden era myth to sell—the romantic Spanish past, humble*

Indians, ruins, gardens, a slower pace of life. From that time on, San Diego was driven by Anglo visions of utopia. The city sold itself as the Spiritual Mecca of Theosophy, a life giving sanitarium for the dying, the Progressive City Beautiful, the Port of the Pacific, America's Finest City, and a sunny tourist theme park. Like Gatsby's mansion, the city is the material manifestation of a colossal illusion. Somehow, it seems to say, you can escape time, history, and maybe even death by transforming space.

PSYCHOGEOGRAPHIC MAP
U.S. / MEXICO BORDER RELOCATION

a vision of a future city by the sea

P. VASQUEZ

5   Joe woke to the sound of an airplane descending into Lindbergh field, laid on his back for a moment and listened to a baby crying, AM talk radio, Norteño music, and a cat rustling in the garbage outside his back window. It was a gloomy day. He got out of bed and walked into his small kitchen to make some coffee. As it brewed, he stared back into the main room at the stacks of books and essays on the floor, his unmade bed, and the picture postcard of Walt Whitman tacked to the wall under the poster of Hieronymous Bosch's "The Temptation of Saint Anthony." When the coffee was done, he walked over to his desk, turned on the computer, and wrote: *"Who is it that stares at me in the mirror? Behind those eyes . . ."* He stopped, shook his head, stared at the screen and tried again: *"Death is at the heart of things. It lies in wait at the center of joy. Behind my eyes, death. In the faces of strangers, death. In the very sinews of things, death. It humbles me with its silence. It is not just death, but a deeper nothing. Sweet death, out of you is born the beating heart. Out of your womb, desire . . ."* The clock radio went off. It was 8:00 A.M.

The morning news said something about a woman giving birth to her child live on an Internet website. Another woman was having her bedroom monitored, twenty-four hours a day by 5,000 people who'd signed up for the "Jody Page." They could see her sleeping, changing, having sex, watching TV. The next story was about a hate crime in East County. A black marine had been stomped to death by four white men who had yelled racial slurs as they brutally murdered him at a barbeque. India and Pakistan had exchanged nuclear threats. One of the leaders of the terrorist group Al Qaeda had issued a *fatwa*. A van full of twelve dead, undocumented immigrants had been found in the desert. Joe clicked off the computer, took off his boxers and went into the bathroom to shower.

As he turned on the water, the radio said it would be sixty-five degrees and cloudy. Traffic was heavy on the 5 and 163 coming into downtown. He got his head wet and the voice told him that the City and the Padres were arguing about money for the new downtown ballpark. The janitors were still on strike and housing prices were going through the roof. He rinsed the shampoo out of his hair and listened to a story about a study that suggested that the club-drug ecstasy destroyed short-term memory function. Wall Street was reaching record highs but the poverty gap persisted. Joe turned off the shower and shook the water out of his hair. A local company was marketing Heaven's Gate suicide cult memorabilia on the Internet. Monks in the Holy Land had turned an ancient monastery into a theme park with a gourmet restaurant. He dried off, walked out of the bathroom, and turned off the radio. He had a few things to do before his afternoon class in San Ysidro, down near the Mexican border.

Joe graded essays for two hours at a coffee house on Laurel and drove over to the park to do some research for his summer class at Central. He had decided to use a new reader about California history and culture, but there was nothing in the book about San

Diego, so he wanted to see what he could find at the local history museum. It was Thursday and the park was fairly empty as Joe drove his '68 Dodge Polara under the arch of the main entrance by the California Building, turned right at the House of Charm, and cruised by the Spreckels Organ Pavilion, out the back way to park his car behind the Space Theater. Joe cut through the lobby of the theater, past a line of tourists waiting to see an OMNIMAX film about dolphins, and walked out of the front door to be greeted by the huge fountain between the theater and the Natural History Museum. He turned left and strolled by Zoro Garden, the site of the Nudist Colony during the 1935 Exposition, and walked through the corridor until he came to the Museum of San Diego History. In the bookstore, they didn't have much but glossy picture books and old copies of the local history journal. Joe leafed through a few issues: Japanese immigrants in the tuna industry, the history of Chicano Park, the Gaslamp's past as a red light district, black theaters in the 1920s, San Diego as a Health Resort, the IWW and the free speech movement, Marcuse at UCSD, the navy during World War II. Maybe he could Xerox a few of these for his students. Joe bought the journals and went downstairs to look at the archives.

Down in the basement, there were old newspapers, letters, maps, and architectural registers, but what interested Joe most were the pictures. He looked at photos of the landscape before the city was built: salt marshes, coastal sage, barren mesas, and oak trees in the foothills. There was photo after photo of places that were no longer there: Little Italy from the harbor to the park, three sanatoriums blocks from his apartment, a Chinatown, a Harlem West, canneries and fleets of tuna boats, a street car line, a baseball field by the harbor, brothels and opium dens in the Stingaree, farmland instead of malls, huge Victorian houses instead of parking lots, canyons instead of freeways. Joe was struck by how many times and how dramatically the city had transformed itself in its fairly short existence. Looking at these pictures gave him an impression of a place in search of itself. He found a reproduction of a picture from 1913. It was an artist's interpretation of what the park would look like after the 1915 Exposition. There was a huge lake under the vine-covered arches of the Laurel Street Bridge. On the shore, idlers strolled by on pastoral walkways. Gondolas covered with garlands of flowers dotted the surface of the placid water, so still it reflected the image of the dream city that rose above it, its Arcadian towers gleaming in the mystical sunlight. It was a no place, out of time. Next to it was a photo of a man in a robot suit holding a nude woman in Zoro Garden. After that, there was a shot of the midget village and a picture of a military ceremony in the Organ Pavilion.

Joe looked at a picture from 1912 of a vigilante crowd beating up a speaker from the Industrial Workers of the World. There were dozens of men struggling to get in a punch or a kick. Behind them, other men were cheering and smiling. Joe had read that Emma Goldman had come to San Diego to support their cause and stayed at the U.S. Grant Hotel until her lover was abducted and she was run out of town. "America's Finest City," Joe thought. He looked at a picture from 1914 of six Native American workers posing with shovels. They were smiling uncomfortably. Three had had their hair cut short and were wearing overalls; three more still had long braids and wore traditional dress. All of their faces were work weary and tired. Joe glanced at his watch, 11:30. It was time to meet his friend Mike Reed downtown.

Mike was the part-timers' representative in the teachers' union at Central College. He also worked as an activist for the San Diego Labor Council and had gone to graduate school with Joe at the University of the Sun. Joe wasn't very active in the teachers' union. He didn't have the stomach for the tedious meetings and conflict, and he didn't have much hope for progressive politics in a town that had tortured Wobblies. Still, he admired Mike's heart and tenacity. Whenever Mike asked him to go to a rally, he went. It was like doing penance for his pessimism. Today he was meeting him at an office tower to help the striking janitor's union picket for an hour. As he drove by the building on B Street, he saw Mike standing by the front entrance, alone, with a "Jobs with Justice" sign. He looked a little beleaguered. Joe parked his car at a meter on 7th, plugged in a few quarters, and ran over to join his friend. Mike smiled as he approached. They shook hands.

"Grab a sign," Mike said.

"My pleasure," replied Joe.

"There should be a few more people here in a little while," Mike explained, "We're trying to cover ten buildings. Can you stay for the rally at 1:00?"

"Have to teach," Joe apologized.

"No problem. Thanks for coming. You have no idea how hard these guys are fighting. There are several people out on a hunger strike and people are on the street twenty-four hours a day," Mike shook his head in wonder and appreciation.

"That's great. I hope they win. What are they asking for?"

"Fifty cents more an hour and health benefits," Mike explained. "That's less than they're asking for in L.A., but you have to be realistic. San Diego is no union town."

People walked by in business suits with hard eyes. Some Italian tourists smiled at them. A family with matching Sea World shirts looked at them in horror as if they were personally responsible for spoiling Sunnyland Theme Park. Joe could hear the janitors chanting "Sí, se puede!" down the street. A few more supporters came and picked up signs. After that, a UPS truck drove up to make a delivery, and when the driver saw the picket line, he honked his horn at them and drove off without stopping.

"Way to go!" Mike yelled, waving and smiling as the truck left. "That's what this town needs," he said to Joe, "Community, solidarity." Joe turned around and looked at the stocky security guard inside the building, glaring at them as he barked into a walkie-talkie. Joe smiled to himself and thought about the picture of the vigilantes beating up the Wobbly.

"Yes it does," he said to Mike, "Absolutely." The janitors down the street were getting louder, "Sí, se puede! Sí, se puede!" Joe overheard a man in a suit grumble, "Fucking speak English." He noticed that Mike had heard too.

"Some people think they own the world," Mike said loudly. The man in the suit raised his arm high and extended his middle finger to Mike without bothering to turn his head.

"Asshole," Joe said. Down the street at another building, he could see a group of janitors running into another office tower with old paint buckets.

"What's up over there?" he asked Mike.

"It's dirt," Mike explained, "They're throwing dirt on the floors of the buildings."

"Good," said Joe, "I like that."

✦ ✦ ✦

Later, on the drive down 5 South to San Ysidro, Joe whizzed by warehouses, shipyards, cheap motels, and wondered if he would call Theresa Sanchez. He pulled into the fast lane and was cut off by a Chevy Suburban. The car radio said the President had apologized for decades of human rights violations in Guatemala. Joe thought about the janitors tossing dirt on the floors of the buildings, imagined them running up the stairs and ransacking offices and boardrooms, dancing on the desks of the technocrats. On the radio, they were talking about day trading. Joe turned it off, made his way over to the slow lane to exit at Dairymart Road, and drove a few blocks to the collection of bungalows that was the "satellite campus" of South Bay College. He parked and walked by the monument to the victims of the mass killing. When this had been a McDonald's, a stranger had walked in the door with a gun and started firing for no apparent reason. He had killed scores of people. Joe had a recurring image of blood streaming onto the floor amidst dropped Big Macs and french fries. He had often wondered if any of the dead had made the dangerous journey across the border from Mexico, only to die in an American fast food restaurant, murdered by an unemployed, alienated Anglo from Dayton, Ohio, who saw them as the perfect target for his unspeakable rage. From an anonymous slum in Mexico City to the nameless celebrity of an American TV tragedy. In the mailroom, there were already twelve essays in his box. Joe grabbed them and headed toward the classroom to collect the remaining eight papers.

Maria Nuncio was there waiting for him with a foil tray of homemade tamales. He thanked her and wished her a nice summer. It was common for his students who were first generation immigrants from Mexico to bring him gifts at the end of the semester. In Mexico, his student Miguel had told him, it's a way to thank the teacher for the gift of knowledge, a sign of respect and reciprocity. In America, Joe thought, everyone assumes it's a bribe. José Rodriquez came in with his essay and a bottle of Kahlua. Joe shook his hand, said goodbye, and watched as he walked out the door into the gray afternoon. Nobody came for a while. He stared at the clock on the back wall, thought about the end of the day, the end of the semester, the way moments of being are closed off, kept from revealing themselves by time. It was 3:30. Marta Almanzar came in with her essay and one of her classmate's. She handed Joe a card with a picture on it of "Flower Day" by Diego Rivera that said only "Thank You." Marta hadn't said a word for sixteen weeks. Joe knew her as a pair of bright attentive eyes. He waited until 4:00, but no one else came. He put the stack of essays into his backpack and headed out across the empty parking lot to his car. The janitor locked the door behind him. Joe decided to drive to the border, park his car, and walk across the line to Tijuana for dinner and a stop at a folk art shop he'd been meaning to visit.

He got back on 5 South briefly, pulled off at the last U.S. exit, and drove another block to a parking lot. As he left his car to make his way across the border, Joe was struck, as always, by the looming presence of *la migra*. There were agents stopping carloads of Latinos to check IDs and ask questions. Cameras and barbed wire sat atop the fences, and the sound of helicopters rose and fell as they circled, lending to the aura of menace. Sometimes, on the way back, Joe would stop midway across the pedestrian bridge and stare at the long crooked fence that divided the two countries, keeping wealth on one side, hunger on the other. You could see people on the Mexican side gathering to make a desperate run past the guards or cutting holes in the fence in the distance. On the other side, there were trucks, guns, helicopters, and high-tech surveillance equipment. Now, as he approached the turnstiles, Joe glanced at the huge reproduction of the Trojan horse straddling the line between the two nations. Small children were running in and out of the long lines of idling cars to hide under the horse's belly. They were chased by Mexican police from one side and American border patrol agents from the other. It was a wry piece of artistic commentary in the midst of a traffic jam. Joe walked by a Mexican man in a Chicago Bulls cap and a Pepsi shirt being led away in handcuffs by two stern, burly blond-haired agents and made his way through the huge clanging metal turnstiles across the line to the Mexican side of the border where the guard station was empty.

Beyond the turnstiles, Joe was greeted by a throng of cab drivers asking if he needed a ride to a brothel, a disco, a pharmacy, or the Jai Alai Palace. He said, "No gracias," four times and walked past a fragile old woman in a *huipile* holding up a McDonald's cup. Joe reached into his pocket, gave her three quarters, and moved on, passing vendors selling ceramic Pooh bears, wool blankets, Guatemalan purses, switch blades, gold earrings, and tie-dyed death skulls with Nazi helmets on. The smell of *carne asada* from the *taquerías* mixed with cigarette smoke drifting over from the outdoor sports book where a crowd of men was standing, staring at TVs with results from Santa Anita, holding Styrofoam cups of coffee, Tecates, and rolled up newspapers.

Joe crossed the street, headed through a commercial courtyard, and walked across the bridge, over the river where the dispossessed had lived in boxes and perished with the winter rains. On the other side, he walked down the stairs by a crowd of small children begging for change. A very small boy of about three ran up and tugged at Joe's pant leg. He gave him his last spare quarter and the band of children followed him for another half block, giggling and yanking at his jeans until they gave up. On the street, the venders were hawking T-shirts, leather goods, birdcages, and laundry baskets, yelling over the rumble of traffic. There were signs for cut-rate Prozac and Cuban cigars. The smells of pastry, smoked meat, exhaust, cologne, thick wool, and new leather filled the air. Joe loved it. He looked up and was taken by the sight of a church steeple in the distance, set off against a deep red sky, burning through the clouds at twilight. At the corner, he looked down the street into the Zona Norte, where the rough bars were, turned left and started toward the folk art store on Avenida Revolucion, the tourist strip. Two drunken gringas in sombreros were having their picture taken with a zebra-striped donkey.

It was still early and the discos were loud and empty. Joe passed by the barkers for a strip show and looked up at a MOTEL sign in the darkening sky, lit up and flashing blue, red, yellow, white, and green. On this corner last December, he had walked out of a bar and been surprised by a Christmas parade, dozens of little angels, all in white dresses with silver tin wings, filling the night with the light of their laughter. Tonight, a truck full of soldiers rolled by looking hard. Joe walked on and the crowd thickened. It was midweek and there were more Mexicans than tourists on the street. Joe's Spanish was weak and the effect was like being outside of language, swimming in sound, sight, and smell. He lost himself in the sea of faces, musing at the mysteries behind their eyes. Even here, on the tourist strip, where the Mexicans sell Americans the prepackaged images they came to see, the street was alive. America was killing the street, but not here, not yet at least. He was full of the life of the world as he wandered into the cluster of shops where he'd seen the art from Oaxaca.

Inside the shop, Joe nodded to the man at the counter and looked at the skeletons carved for *Día de los Muertos*: Death as a doctor performing surgery, Death shooting baskets, Death as a rich woman in fine dress, Death waving from the window of an SUV, Death watching TV, Death drinking tequila, Death doing aerobics in a pink leotard. Joe strolled down the aisle and looked at a reproduction of a print by José Guadalupe Posada of Death addressing skulls and skeletons in a graveyard. Death was gesturing like a preacher, mesmerizing them with the powerful stare emanating from his empty eye sockets. In the background, a streetcar full of happy tourist skeletons was just pulling into the graveyard wearing hollow smiles. Joe moved on to a row of black-and-white tissue-paper banners picturing Death on a bicycle, Death getting married, Death dancing, and Death working a stove. Next to these, was a table full of brightly colored purple, red, and yellow paper maché skulls, model *ofrendas* made of pottery, and a stack of postcard prints. Joe glanced at one featuring a pompous, fat politician with a bag of money, running in fear from a cackling skeleton that was closing in quickly, inevitably. Joe had read Octavio Paz's description of the Day of the Dead as a ritual where "death revenges us against life," mocking human power, vanity, and pretension. What also struck Joe was the wonderful sense of humor and play. Death informs us of our absurdity, he thought. Joe walked back over to the small, carved figures and remembered reading that in Aztec mythology human mortality was the result of an accident. If the Plumed Serpent had not dropped the bones of our ancestors, humans would be immortal. Joe preferred this to the Master Plan of his Catholic background. He picked up a carving of Death sitting at a desk behind a typewriter, a cigarette burning in an ashtray off to the side. He walked over to the counter and handed it to the storekeeper.

"You like?" he said.

"Sí," said Joe.

"Bueno, cinco dólares." The man smiled at Joe and wrapped the figure very slowly and carefully in white tissue paper before putting it in a little yellow bag. Joe looked at the man's thick fingers, covered with tiny scars.

"Gracias," Joe said as he took the bag.

"De nada."

Out on Revolución again, Joe stopped at a stand and ordered two fish tacos, ate them quickly, and walked down a side street toward Constitución to a little bar he knew. He moved seamlessly through the stream of human atoms drifting like shadows on the unlit street. Inside the bar, it was dark and empty except for the bartender. He ordered a Negra Modelo and the old woman brought it to him silently, sullenly took his money, and sat down to finish watching a *telenovela*. Joe had a sip of beer, took the figure out of the bag, unwrapped it, and set it on the counter. In the dim red light of the bar, Death smiled at him from behind a typewriter. He could die now, he thought, and it wouldn't matter. He was a stranger here, a stranger at home, a stranger to himself. Everything seemed to fall away from him. He laughed at himself, quietly. He felt totally alone in the world and, inexplicably, happy.

6 Pete stumbled out of the bathroom in the dim cantina and squinted in the smoky darkness. He didn't see Randy, shit. They had been drinking for hours and he wasn't sure where he was or how to get back to the border and back to the base. He walked over to the bar, sat down and ordered another Dos Equis. Randy would come back, he thought. Where could he have gone? They could get in big trouble coming down here against Navy rules. Still, nobody they'd known had been caught. It had been a good night so far, winning a few hundred on the Lakers at the Jai Alai Palace, wandering from bar to bar in the Zona Norte. Pete had never been here before. It struck him as dirty, dangerous, and exhilarating all at the same time. There were no rules here; you could do anything.

A woman that looked like a man in lipstick sat down on the stool next to him and grabbed his crotch. Pete chugged his beer, got up and walked out of the bar. He pulled his watch out of his pocket. It was 3:40 A.M. The street was still teeming with people. Pete walked by some taco stands and a guy tried to lure him into an alley. He shook his head and walked into a disco full of men in cowboy hats, where the women all sat on a bench by the wall, waiting for someone to dance with them. It reminded Pete of a high school dance back in Georgia. He looked around, hoping to see Randy. No luck. He bought himself a shot of tequila, slammed it, and walked back out, past a storefront church, a hotel lobby, another taco stand. Pete felt like he'd been walking in circles all night. He didn't recognize anything. He walked into a bar full of tables, occupied by couples in nice evening clothes. There was a porno movie on the television behind the bar. He ordered another shot, no Randy. Next he poked his head in a bar full of men in red dresses, moved on to a strip club where they served tiny beers and comics came on before each girl danced. It reminded Pete of pictures he'd seen of nightclubs in the fifties. He bought a small beer, watched a girl dance. She didn't take off her top. Pete finished his beer as a new comic came on. He couldn't understand a word he was saying. He waved off a new beer, left, and bought a pack of Mexican cigarettes from a stand in the street. It was amazing, Pete thought. I just point and hold up money and everything gets done. Easy.

Pete stuck his head inside a pool hall, still no Randy. He turned the corner, walked down another street and into a strip club. No Randy, no Americans period. He hadn't seen an American face for a while now. He sat down and a man brought a beer on a tray. The women actually stripped here. Pete watched a fat girl with really big ones. He ordered a shot of tequila. "To-kill-ya," he said. A woman sat down next to him, smiled, and grabbed at his crotch. He didn't resist. She ordered herself a shot and he paid for it. The next thing he knew, he was walking up the stairs of a cheap hotel. A stern old woman took ten dollars from him, handed the girl a condom, and looked at him with hate in her eyes. Pete walked to a small room with the girl. His head was spinning. He lit a cigarette, gave her one, and really looked at her for the first time. She was young, about nineteen. Her face was round and sweet.

"Twenty bucks," she said.

"You speak English," Pete said in surprise. She didn't answer.

When she took off her clothes, Pete saw that she was thin and shapely. Her dark brown skin was drowned in strong perfume. She went down on him first, and it took a while for the feeling to cut through the liquor. She shook it roughly a few times, exasperated. When he was hard she put on the condom, pushed him on his back, climbed on top, and rode him efficiently with no expression on her face. Pete tried to kiss her, but she turned her face away silently, rode him harder, harder, and he came. She rinsed off in the tiny shower and was dressed almost as quickly as Pete could stand up to walk into the bathroom and pull off the condom.

"Thank you," he said dumbly. She didn't answer, shutting the door behind her as she left. Pete wiped himself with a tissue, got dressed, and walked downstairs. The street was pitch dark and he didn't even see it coming when the punch came. Pain shot up through his nose, flooding his skull as he landed hard on his back, felt the hands, rustling through his pockets. Pete took a feeble swing but he could already hear the sound of feet running away down an alley. He lay there a while and felt his pockets. Whoever it was had gotten it all but ten dollars rolled in a ball in his left pocket. Pete got up, walked back toward the street with the lights. He could taste the blood pouring into his mouth, thick, salty. He walked into a bar on the corner, sat down and ordered a tequila shot. The bartender shook his head in amusement, gave him a bar towel, and poured him a shot. Pete wiped the blood off his face with the dirty towel and drank the shot. The pain had brought his head back to him. Where the fuck did Randy go, he wondered. He checked his watch, 5:30 A.M. New light was pouring in under the door. The lights inside the bar were turned up.

"Time to go, my friend," said the bartender. Pete nodded and walked outside. The street was bathed in the ethereal pink and yellow light of dawn. Two yawning women in bright blue and red dresses were standing quietly, waiting for their food to cook at a taco stand just outside the door. There were Indian children sleeping on the ground under colorful wool blankets, and the smoke rose from the grill like a soul ascending toward heaven. Pete stood for a moment in the beautiful stillness, full of shame and wonder. It was like nothing he had ever seen before.

7

Hortencia sat on the edge of the bed and smoked as the first light of dawn came in through the window of her shabby hotel room. She had done well tonight, two-hundred dollars. That was more than she could make in a month at her old job. If she kept saving, maybe she could buy a boutique back in Guadalajara. It was not so bad, she thought, not as bad as it felt. Some of the men were pigs, ugly and mean. They would hit her and try to do it without paying. They wouldn't want to use the rubber. Tonight a man tried to stick it in her ass without asking. She kicked him hard in the stomach, like a mule, and he ran out without getting any. "*Pendejo*," she said to herself and laughed. Once he was gone, she had locked the door, taken a shower, and tried to wash his touch off of her, scrubbing so hard that it had made her skin red. Other men were not so bad. They would be too drunk and get embarrassed. They would finish fast and look shy. They would act like she was a girlfriend and try to kiss her.

The crystal was wearing off and the weight of the liquor was making her heavy. She felt her heart beating, lay back on the bed, and began to cry quietly. Her mother would die if she knew. In her last letter, Hortencia had told her that she was working as a maid in a tourist hotel. Tourists! Most of the men were Americans, fucking rich Americans! She thought about the boy who had tried to kiss her tonight. She had thought for a moment that he was all right. Just a drunken Navy boy. She had started to feel nice, but something in his blue eyes stopped her. They made her feel cold and dead inside. If she had had a knife, she would have stabbed him in the heart, she thought, stabbed him again and again, and watched his thick red blood pour out of his wounds as he groaned.

Jack Mosby with a Wobbly comrade, Tijuana, Mexico, 1911.
Courtesy of the San Diego Historical Society.

8   *In 1911, during the Mexican Revolution, as Pancho Villa, Emiliano Zapata, and their army of the dispossessed were battling to overthrow Porfirio Díaz in the heart of Mexico, a smaller battle raged in the North of the country. The Industrial Workers of the World, seeing a chance to make real their dream of a classless society with no bosses, laid siege on one of Mexico's small border towns. Their army was composed of socialists, anarchists, and drifters. They were hoboes who'd ridden the rails across America, hopping from job to job—ex-pickers, lumber jacks, rock miners, sailors, farm hands, dock workers, and outlaws who were sick of doing shit work, sick of taking orders. As the preamble to the IWW's constitution said: "The working class and the employing class have nothing in common. There can be no peace so long as hunger and want are found among millions of the working people and the few, who make up the employing class, have all the good things in life. Between these two classes a struggle must go on until the workers of the world organize as a class, take possession of the means of production, abolish the wage system, and live in harmony with the Earth. . . . We are forming the structure of the new society within the shell of the old." The concept of borders and nations meant nothing to them.*

   "The undesirable citizens of the U.S. are with you heart and soul," Jack London wrote to the rebels in Mexico, "We are not respectable.

Neither are you." Led by U.S. Marine deserter, Jack Mosby, and ex-British army fighter Caryl Pryce, the Wobbly army took Tijuana in a bloody battle at dawn and a red flag rose above the city that read, "Tierra y Libertad." It was May tenth. For a little over a month, the Wobblies held the town, dreaming of freedom, bread, and roses, but on June twenty-second, the Mexican army responded and headed north from Ensenada. Mosby led the Wobblies south to meet them and the battle was lost in only hours. The rebels fled back across the border. Mosby was arrested for desertion and was shot trying to escape. Pryce, who had deserted his comrades before the battle, went to Hollywood to act in westerns.

9 It was 9:00 P.M., Thursday night and Joe was at Central College in Room 113, gathering together the stack of his students' final essays, and getting ready to leave. Theresa hadn't stopped by as he had hoped she would. There was nothing from Laila Washington, no word from Bob Anderson. Joe put the stack in his backpack, walked up the stairs in the dark to check his mailbox one last time. There was a small white envelope addressed to Mr. Professor Blake. It was from Bob Anderson: *"How do you know what I know? People like you with your poems and books. Do you know I see the light around you? You have a light around you and colors you can't see. I'm like Shakespeare's genius with the torture of demons. Can't finish when they won't let me. People like you always trying to fuck with my mind. Your day will come. Will it be redemption? They drag me deep down in a hole. I see things you can't see. There is light* around you, green and yellow and red. Why are you torturing my mind? The blood of the masters will run down the palace walls. Will it be redemption? I see the light around you. Why are you killing my mind? I can see things, things you don't know." Joe sighed, tossed the letter in a trashcan, and walked out of the mailroom across the deserted campus toward Twelfth Avenue where it turns into Park Boulevard. His load was light tonight so he had walked instead of driving. Joe knew Bob must have gone off his meds, but something about the note shook him to the core. There was a kind of furious, desperate energy in it. It was a mind grasping for something to hold on to, a soul fleeing from un-nameable horror. Joe walked by San Diego High School, crossed the street, passed over the freeway, and hit the edge of the park.

Joe could see bodies scattered on the grass under the trees and wondered if one of them was Bob. First his job, then his house, and finally his mind. There was a brutal symmetry to the process of Bob's descent. Joe walked on and approached a bus bench where a man was sleeping. As he neared it, he recognized the gaunt pale face of Bob Anderson under a wrinkled Padres cap. Joe leaned over him and noticed a bad cut on the bridge of his nose. He was thinner and smelled of urine. Joe touched his shoulder gently and Bob lurched to an upright position and stared at him with anger and fear. Joe started to speak to him, but before he could utter a sound, Bob pushed him violently to the ground, grunted, and screamed, "Assassin!" before running off into the park. Joe watched him disappear into the darkness, picked himself up off the ground and continued on. Bob was lost, utterly lost.

Dazed, Joe walked past the Space Theater and into the park. The big fountain was lit up beautifully, spouting a huge stream of illuminated water into the night sky. Joe listened to the sound of it surging and falling. There was no one to be seen on the Prado, but the buildings were bathed in an ethereal golden light. Joe walked through the courtyard of the Casa del Prado to the reflecting pool. He stopped and gazed at the gently glowing image of the Casa de Balboa crowned by the moon on the still water. It was a strange dream palace beckoning him to descend. Joe took in the silence, let it slice through him. There was no solace in it. He thought about a line in Bob Anderson's note, "Will it be redemption?" Joe walked out of the park, over the bridge toward Fifth Avenue. What was redemption? He didn't know.

Back in his studio, Joe sat down at his computer and wrote: *"Are there some kinds of suffering from which there is no redemption? Can we be so lost, so utterly alone in the world that we lose our connection to the greater self? Naked in the brutal dark, a stranger even to yourself. Is it freedom to stop clinging to the world or is it helpless, terrifying drift? What do I know of horror in my warm room with food in my belly? Why should I be so lucky to know small joys? Why am I too not wretched and forlorn? What do I really know? Part of me is with him in the dark night of his soul."* Joe stopped, read what he had written, sighed, shook his head and erased it. He turned off the computer, undressed, and clicked on the small TV on the table next to his bed. There was a smug talking head on *Nightline* crowing about the triumph of the new economy. Joe picked up the remote to change the channel, lay back on his bed and surfed: phone sex, a rerun of a Padres' loss, right-wing political commentary, mean spirited late night comedy. He stopped for a minute to look at a documentary on the search for the giant squid in the unknown depths of the ocean. No one had ever seen one alive. He flipped past the food channel, the animal channel, the history channel, the classic sports channel, the religious channel, two music channels, a Mexican game show, the Home Shopping Network. Finally, he stopped at CNN, put down the flipper, closed his eyes, and listened to the TV tell him about a police shooting in New York City, a celebrity wedding, and the stock market. A voice said that Generation X was all washed up by age thirty-five. The real movers and shakers were dot.com twenty-somethings with money to burn who were investing heavily in real estate. Joe was thirty-five.

He fell asleep and dreamed of Bob Anderson slipping into a bottomless hole, barely holding on with one hand, reaching up desperately, feebly with the other. Joe went over to the edge of the pit and took the hand that suddenly, inexplicably, was full of strength and trying to pull him down into the yawning chasm. Joe looked into Bob's eyes and they were full of menace. He struggled to stay up, but he was losing ground, his head slowly descending toward Bob's face. Joe could hear the moans of the unseen echoing up from the pit. Just as he was about to fall in, Bob stopped pulling, lost strength, and kissed him gently on the forehead, his eyes now full of sorrow as he fell backwards into the ocean of nothingness. Joe woke up with a start and a voice was saying that profits were reaching record levels. He turned off the TV and laid back, his heart still beating fiercely.

10   Bob woke up with the morning light and crawled out from under the bush where he'd taken refuge after the attack. He coughed deeply as he stood up, not bothering to brush the dirt and leaves from his hair and clothing. He had a kind of jagged energy. Something told him to walk. He wandered out of the park towards downtown, passed over the freeway bridge, wincing at the roar that rose from below. A car honked at him as he crossed A Street, not noticing the red light. At C Street, he stopped in the middle of the trolley tracks and watched the red thing cut into the city. The trolley cop moved him on and he made it to Broadway, turned right for some reason, and tried the door of a dead bar under a closed-down pool hall. Further on, he noticed the smell of eggs and bacon, walked into a cheap diner, and tried to sit down. The man behind the counter pointed to the door angrily and reached for a baseball bat under the counter. Bob turned and left, walked a few more blocks past an empty bar, an Internet cafe full of the smell of muffins, a place that sold old things. He turned right, crossed against another red, and the moving things honked and cursed. Why did they hate him?

It was the time of day when the people came. They were parking in lots and filling the sidewalks, walking fast, holding cups, and carrying suitcases. Nobody looked at him. The people stepped out of his way. He crossed another street behind a group of them, turned left, and came to a huge glass tower. This was the place where the masters lived. They hid in these places behind mirrored glass and controlled things. Bob stopped in front of the door and watched the people streaming in. One of them was talking into his hand. Bob stared at him. A voice said, "Get out of here!" He hated them. Why did they torture him so? Bob lumbered a few feet away from the door and noticed that if he walked into the shadows he could see them inside, concealed in cubicles, hunched over keyboards, gazing at screens. He stepped back and screamed at the tower, "Look at yourselves! Look at yourselves! What are you hiding from! I know things you can't know! I see the light around you!" The walking people gave him a wider berth. A woman in a dark coat stopped and gawked at him. Bob took out his penis and urinated on the mirrored glass. A big man in a red jacket came, pushed him, and barked, "I'm calling the cops, asshole!" Bob put it back in and walked on.

Bob thought he remembered places, but they weren't there. A place that used to be a hot dog stand, a hotel that was a bank. Bob hit a dead end, turned left, and wandered past Golden Hall. The people all hated him. No one would look at him. Big cars were pulling into the driveway of a fancy hotel. Bob tried to walk into the lobby to sit in a nice chair, and look at the chandeliers, but a man in a suit with a headset on pointed to the door sternly and spoke into his microphone. Why were they torturing him? He crossed the street to Horton Plaza Park where there were plants in pots surrounded by chains. Bob thought he remembered grass. He looked at the pretty fountain. He felt like lying down again. After only a minute, a policeman kicked the bottom of his shoe and told him to move on. The policeman spoke into his hand as he watched him leave. Bob headed into Horton Plaza, walked up the stairs and wandered in circles. There was nice music. No one would let him come

48

in. He could smell cookies, french fries, and cinnamon rolls. Bob didn't know who he was. He went up an escalator and walked in another circle. There were different pictures of fruit on the walls. Bob saw books, dresses, football jerseys, movie posters, painted plates, and many bright things in the windows. Everything mixed together. He thought he was touching himself but a woman screamed. Another man with a headset came and escorted him roughly out of the mall.

Bob walked down Fourth Avenue toward Market. People were speaking different languages. The buildings were old and full of decorations. It looked like Disneyland. Bob smelled toast. He hit Market, crossed the street, turned left, walked a block, and stopped outside the window of a store that sold wigs. There was a bright yellow wig that he liked. He wanted a bright yellow wig. The woman in the store wouldn't let him come in. His feet hurt badly, but he kept walking, zigzagging east of Market, not paying attention to where he was. At one point, he paused by a fence where they had blown up a building. Nothing was there but dirt now. Bob stood and watched the loud machines. Things used to be there. He thought he remembered a place where he used to sleep. He walked past the area where the fence was and wandered several more blocks to an old wooden house. It looked familiar. Bob sat on the steps and rested. The rest felt nice, but a voice yelled, "I thought I told you never to come back!" Everyone hated him, Bob thought. He walked on. It was a beautiful morning, sunny and bright.

11 It was Friday, 5:00 P.M. sharp and Janey turned off her computer, put her desk in order, and briskly walked out of the office saying "bye-bye" to her coworkers as she hurried past them on her way to the elevator. During the elevator trip, she turned down an invitation to go to happy hour in the Gaslamp, and pulled at the hem of her skirt. She didn't like the Gaslamp. It was too crowded, a little sketchy after dark. In the lobby, she said "bye-bye" twice more, walked out the main entrance, across the street towards the parking lot and her cherry red Jeep Grand Cherokee. There was a homeless man sitting on the bus bench next to the lot. He was filthy, sunburned, and totally gross. She noticed that he was talking to himself loudly: "I can see the light around you!" he said. Janey did not make eye contact.

She took out her keys and hit the button on the device that turned off her car alarm. It beeped twice. Mimi had suggested she stop in Hillcrest at the Organic Gourmet to get some ahi on special, but she didn't feel like it. The last time she went there, she'd seen two men kissing in the parking lot. She knew it wasn't politically correct, but it bothered her. Janey fixed her lipstick in the rear view mirror and started up the engine. She headed straight for Interstate 5, listening to Raging Robert on the radio as she checked for messages on her cell phone. As soon as she got on the freeway, she felt lighter. Raging Robert was warning her about the illegal invasion at the border and calling for armed civilian Patriot Patrols. "The liberals will call us racist vigilantes," he said, "But history will remember us as the heroes who saved America and the liberals as traitors who sought to subvert her." Janey nodded firmly to herself, checked her cell phone again, and sent a text message to her husband. She continued her crawl towards North County, laughed at Robert's funny joke about "Billary Clinton" and listened intently as he turned to sticking it to the big union fat cats for stealing her tax dollars for their gold-plated pensions. Why do they deserve special treatment? she thought. Couldn't they put money in a 401k like she did? Finally she exited onto the clean, wide street near her neighborhood, stopped at the giant Ralph's for some chardonnay and boneless, skinless chicken breasts, picked up an old Mel Gibson movie at Blockbuster, and cruised down side streets with no sidewalks towards her nice new peach Santa Fe style home, just like the one next door.

Wobbly street speaker on soap box, San Diego, 1911.
Courtesy of the San Diego Historical Society.

12　　　*Fresh from a victory in a free speech campaign in Fresno, the Wobblies came to San Diego in 1911. The city had passed an ordinance banning street meetings downtown, and the fifty local Wobblies, along with a coalition of other progressive groups, formed a Free Speech League to combat it. Soon, five thousand Wobblies from across the nation flooded the town, parading, protesting, and filling the jails. The oligarchy's response was immediate and brutal. They encouraged the formation of a vigilante army to patrol the county line and to beat and terrorize the Wobblies. The police attacked protesters with fire hoses, tortured and murdered prisoners in jail. "These people do not belong to any country, no flag, no laws, no Supreme Being," railed Police Chief J. Ken Wilson. "Listen to them singing," he bemoaned, "They are singing all the time, and yelling and hollering, and telling the jailors to quit work and join the union. They are worse than animals." The Union ran an editorial suggestion from the vigilantes: "We propose to keep up the deportation of these undesirable citizens as fast as we can catch them, and hereafter they will not only be carried to the county line and dumped there, but we intend to leave our mark on them in the shape of tar rubbed into their hair, so that a shave will be necessary to remove it, and this is what* these agitators (all of them) may expect from now on, that the outside world may know that they have been to San Diego."

On a fine day in March, a drunken vigilante army of four hundred men armed with rifles, pistols, and pickaxe handles stopped a train carrying 150 Wobblies. The vigilantes were realtors, shopkeepers, clerks, and ranchers; frightened middle-class men, more afraid of the poor than the rich. Stomp them down, they thought, and keep what we have. The vigilantes herded their new prisoners into a cattle corral and beat them all night. The Wobblies were made to run a gauntlet of one hundred men who struck them with fists, boots, and pick ax handles. They broke their bones and bloodied their faces, made them kiss the American flag. The Tribune responded with an editorial about the Wobblies: "Hanging is none too good for them. They would be much better off dead, for they are absolutely useless in the human economy; they are the waste matter of creation and should be drained off into the sewer of oblivion, there to rot in cold obstruction like any other excrement."

In the midst of this orgy of hate and terror, Emma Goldman came to San Diego to lecture on Ibsen. When Goldman, the champion of free love and anarchist revolution, arrived in the city with her lover, Ben Reitman, a vigilante crowd of women greeted her and tried to pull her from her car as they screamed, "We will strip her naked! We will tear out her guts!" At the U.S. Grant Hotel, she was met by Mayor James Wadham, who said of the vigilantes across the street, "You hear that mob? They mean business." Goldman refused the Mayor's offer of safe passage out of town and instead asked to speak to the crowd from an open window upstairs. The Mayor refused. She returned to her room to find that Reitman had been abducted. Goldman was told that he had been put on a train to Los Angeles by the vigilantes. She took the 2:45 A.M. train north. Reitman had been stripped naked, beaten, tarred and feathered. The vigilantes had pushed a cane up his rectum and twisted his testicles violently. They forced him to sing

"The Star Spangled Banner" and kiss the flag. They burned "IWW" into his ass with cigar butts. Finally, he ran the gauntlet, each man getting in a kick or a punch. When he was reunited with Goldman, she helped him undress and treated his wounds. The *Union* celebrated the news: "Emma Goldman, anarchist leader and defender of the I.W.W. is speeding on her way to Los Angeles and her manager, Dr. Ben Reitman, is said to be somewhere on his way to Los Angeles, clad thinly in his underwear and a coat of tar and feathers acquired somewhere on the Penasquitos Ranch twenty miles to the north of this city after being forced to kneel and kiss the Stars and Stripes and promise solemnly never to return to San Diego."

13

Joe was dreaming in Technicolor of sitting by the window of an empty white apartment that glowed with a ghostly light. He was watching planes crash. They came in, one after the other, and either hit the ground producing deep red flames or exploded midair like fluorescent fireworks, popping into wonderful blue and yellow flowers that slowly faded and fell just as the next plane went off. All of this was occurring against a pitch-black sky with no city lights, no stars. Joe felt a profound peace as he watched the spectacle, a calm at the eye of the storm. He woke up to the sound of a big jet cruising into Lindbergh, smiled, and got up to make coffee. It was 9:00 A.M. Monday, the first day of his week off before the summer session started. He felt light as he ate a banana, poured his coffee, and walked over to his computer to write:

I do not know what redemption is but I seek it—
Looking into the face of madness and guessing the meaning of
    dreams;
Walking through city streets, watching the strangers, and loving the
    dance of
        the height of the day;
Reading the paper in a neighborhood diner, eavesdropping
    whenever I can;
Listening to the music of a foreign tongue, not knowing what
    anything means;
Driving through desert as the sun fades to evening, feeling alone
    in the world;
Making love in a strange room, so long and intensely that it feels
    like a trading of souls.
And if this does not save me, then perhaps just a minute more to
    ponder the
        nature of non-being;
To remember vision through the eyes of a child;
To hear deeply into music, then sound;
To feel the rough edges of things;
To give into anger and yield to forgiveness;
To see myself through the eyes of a stranger;
To just be;
To pray without praying;
To dream a whole life in a minute;
To awaken to the rebirth of desire.
And if this too falls short, then grant me just one second more of
    diving deeply

into the texture of things—air, earth, water, fire, objects
made and worn by hands;
Of holding myself on the edge of abandon;
Of swimming in the center of delight;
Of the spark of passion in beautiful eyes;
Of the warm touch of skin—lips, nipples, stomachs, thighs;
Of a slant of ethereal light;
Of seeing the crowd as a family of being—feeling connected to a
myriad of
strangers;
Of sudden and welcome revelation;
Of finding myself by losing myself;
Of looking long out my window at the skyline at night,
wondering and yearning for what
I don't know;
There are not words for everything
I desire
and adore.

It was a start, Joe thought, maybe he could do something with it. If only there was more time. Still, he felt good. He shut down the computer, turned on the radio and took a shower. The first story was an in-depth focus on a hate crime in North County. A group of migrant workers had been beaten and shot by a gang of young white men in a camp near Black Mountain Road in Carmel Valley. The migrants, many of whom were in their sixties, had been assaulted for hours. Eight white males with closely cropped hair drove up to the camp in a sports utility vehicle bearing pellet guns. They sprayed the men with gunfire, pelted them with rocks, hunted them down, and beat them with pipes, all the while screaming racial slurs. One of them yelled: "Go back to Mexico," in broken Spanish. The migrants said the young men were big and had military haircuts.

Sixty-one-year-old José Fuentes told the reporter, "They were playing with me. They were hunting me like a rabbit. They threw rocks at me like I was an animal." When the gunfire started he said, "All I could hear was the sound of the trigger. I didn't want to show my face because I didn't want them to leave me blind." Joe shook the water out of his hair. He felt vaguely sick as he listened. It reminded him of the black marine who'd been beaten and stomped to death at a party in Poway. Joe also thought of the reading he'd done yesterday about the vigilante mobs during the free speech battles here, and the vicious attacks on farm workers in the Imperial Valley in the thirties. The weather was going to be partly cloudy. He turned off the radio, got dressed, and sat down on his bed. It was 11:00 A.M. He decided to call Theresa Sanchez.

Theresa wasn't home so he left a message: "Hi, it's Joe. I'd like to see you." He hated the sound of his own voice on the phone. Joe hung up, grabbed his wallet, and headed out of his studio. In the hallway, he could smell pot smoke and bacon grease. There was a transvestite with a five o'clock shadow getting into the elevator. A couple was fighting in the apartment by the door. Joe walked out onto Fifth Avenue and squinted in the sunlight as he turned left on Hawthorne, went a block, and jogged across Sixth Avenue to walk along the park toward downtown. The hillside leading up to Marston point was framed by eucalyptus and palm trees and covered with a carpet of lush green grass and white daisies. Joe hit the freeway bridge, passed a homeless man pushing a shopping cart, gazed up at the El Cortez Hotel on the hill above the interstate. The old landmark had been closed for years, but now it was an expensive condo complex, serving as one of the anchors of the aggressive gentrification of downtown. Joe had tried to walk into the lobby once. He was met by a pissy security guard who told him he was in a "private space," but that guided tours were available "by appointment." Joe walked on, glanced across the street at Saint Cecilia's, an old church that was now a theater, crossed Cedar, Beech, and Ash, strolling by lawyer's offices, language schools, copy stores, pizza places, and bail bonds joints.

At A Street, Joe stopped at a red light and looked over at the old Harcourt, Brace, and Jovanovich building that was now the World Trade Center. It was white with blue trimming, like a Modernist wedding cake. When the light changed, he crossed A and walked alongside the huge, ugly glass and concrete tower that was the Comerica Bank building. The pedestrian traffic was picking up now as people streamed out of the office buildings to have lunch as if they'd been freed from jail. Joe noticed a lot of nods to bohemia amidst the mostly white crowd: a secretary with a diamond nose stud, business men in black suits with shaved heads and earrings, neat little pony tails, funky sunglasses, tattoos peeking out from slit skirts and rolled up shirtsleeves. There were nods to punk, post-punk, goth, hippie, lounge, hip-hop and rave culture. Hip is dead, Joe thought; the organizational man has e-mail, a cell phone, an SUV, and counter-cultural fashion sense. Even the older workers wore jeans sometimes. Only the smokers looked stressed and guilty, standing in doorways like pale outcasts of a fascist health club. He smiled at a pretty woman with long, curly red hair and Kokopeli earrings in a white T-shirt and a purple and blue Indian print skirt, carrying coffee and a copy of the Tao Te Ching. He thought he saw something in her eyes. She carefully ignored him.

Joe moved on, glanced at the mural poking up over the Roman-esque roof of the Southern Hotel. It was a *San Diego Union-Tribune* headline that read "America's Finest City." Joe crossed B Street, smirked to himself as he remembered reading how that name had been coined to make San Diego feel better after the city had lost the Republican Convention in 1972. He passed by the chic Sixth Avenue Bistro that used to be McDonald's and the lobby of the Southern Hotel where a solitary old man sat, sadly reading the paper on a straight-backed wooden chair. The front desk was closed, no rooms available. Joe passed a Mexican place, a drugstore, the Kebob House. Lots of the old stores and restaurants were closed down or closing. New places were under construction. Joe crossed the trolley tracks at C Street and gave a quarter to an old woman with no teeth in a Chargers jersey. He passed a coffee stand and more construction sites, looked across at a dead Woolworth's, hit Broadway and turned left. The office crowd disappeared as Joe strolled by Superfly Tattoo, Cortez Jewelry, and a language school. European tourists mingled with rooming house residents on the sidewalk. There were hotel workers, maids, and security guards in uniforms waiting at the bus stop. Joe walked past a Chinese Buffet, crossed Seventh Avenue, went by the 99 Cent Store and hit Wahrenbrock's Book House next to the Dim Sum Kingdom.

Joe nodded to the man behind the counter and walked up the dusty old wooden steps to the third floor where the San Diego section was at the top of the stairway. The dark musty quiet of the bookstore stood in stark contrast to the bustling street. It took a while for his eyes to adjust to the dim light. There was another room to the right and a half-opened door. Joe imagined secret rooms and passageways full of mystery. Once he could see, he looked over old maps of the city, histories of Balboa Park, a biography of Alonzo Horton, self-published books about the Stingaree and Wyatt Earp. Joe picked up a used copy of *The Journal of San Diego History* with an architectural guide to the Gaslamp Quarter and noticed a whole row of novels by Max Miller: *I Cover the Waterfront, Mexico Around Me, A Stranger Came to Port,* and *The Man on the Barge.* He read the jacket descriptions and discovered that they were all thirties novels. Miller was San Diego's second-rate Hemingway. Joe loved the charcoal drawings on the covers, the yellowed pages, and the smell of the past. He opened *The Man on the Barge* to the middle and read a passage:

Out here on the barge at night he felt off the world somehow. He was not of it. He felt as though he never would die, or had died already. He was not quite sure, nor did it matter. The water between him and the mainland formed a separation more mysterious than merely two miles of sea. The water could as well have been a void, a nothingness, and he was suspended beyond it.

For Miller, it seemed, San Diego Harbor was at the end of the earth, a last resort. It seemed interesting. Joe kept it, grabbed *A Stranger Came to Port* as well, and walked downstairs to the counter to buy them. "I haven't sold one of these for years," the owner told him.

Joe walked out of the store, stood onto the sidewalk for a second, and decided to turn left. He passed the Afrocentric Barber and a luggage store, crossed Eighth Avenue, and went by an empty Internet coffee house and the New Cafe, where the smell of egg rolls and Kung Pao chicken was flooding out onto the street. He noticed that Beanie's Lobby was open next door and strolled into the bar. It smelled of decades of cigarette smoke and stale beer. There were three sullen, silent barflies manning stools and nursing long necks. The bartender was reading the sports page and smoking. A staticky TV was showing the Padres game with no sound, and no one was watching. Joe sat down and ordered a Bud. The bartender brought it to him silently and took the money. "Thanks," Joe said. There was no reply. This was like the last bar on earth, Joe thought, smiling to himself. Downtown had been filled with hundreds of these places about a decade ago. Now there were only a few dives left. Joe wondered how long the Lobby had until it became a fern bar. He took a sip of his beer and began to read in the dim smoky light.

A Stranger Came to Port was about a businessman named Hardson who had run away from his job and family in Minneapolis, Minnesota, and "disappeared" to live on a houseboat in San Diego Harbor with a scavenger named Lobster Johnny. As Joe read on, he discovered that Hardson had had it with social niceties and obligations. Hardson was also sick of unions and FDR. He had escaped to a houseboat to watch the world go by, but had then decided to go fishing with a tuna boat. He admired the fact that *"fisherman alone remain the true link to the old days when all men were hunters."* The problem today, Hardson thought, was that the inferior man was running things and punishing those who had shown the initiative to get ahead. A bit of a Social Darwinist, this Hardson, Joe thought. But just as Joe was about to put the book down, Hardson was contemplating nothingness like an Existentialist: *"He could not comprehend nothingness. What was nothingness?"* Joe took a slug of his beer and read about Hardson thinking that *"All men are part of each other."* A few pages later he sounded Buddhist, then misogynist, and back to Social Darwinist. Hardson/Miller had a problem with philosophical consistency. But what struck Joe the most was the sense of aimlessness, desperation, and drift. It was as if one of the cranky retired fishermen who went to The Waterfront Bar and Grill had written a novel expressing all their unarticulated disdain and yearning. The government had killed the tuna fleets, but they had seen things, "Let me tell ya." Joe stopped after a passage where Hardson had pondered his loss of ambition. He finished his beer and walked out of the bar, back to his studio to check his messages.

Back in his studio, Joe was happy to hear the voice of Theresa Sanchez on the phone. She could see him next Saturday after her shift if he could pick her up at the bookstore where she worked in Old Town. Joe called back and left a message that he could. There was also a message from his friend Christine in Ohio. She had come out to school here with him back in the late eighties, but had gotten a job back home at Black Swamp State just south of Toledo. Joe called her and they talked. She told him stories about Black Swamp. A man who thought he was Jesus Christ went into the local bar and ordered a Martini and charged it to Yaweh. The man then walked across town to the Ford dealership and told them he was

Christ in the form of Jim Thome, power hitter for the Cleveland Indians. Finally, our Lord ended up on his front porch pouring bleach on himself as the police arrived. He was nude and told the police he was trying to clean off his whiteness. Another man posing as a team doctor for the college football team went to the homes of eight local families and gave their sons, all of whom had hopes of pulling a scholarship, proctology exams, until one boy's mother asked why such an exam was necessary. Upon being questioned, the man fled into a cornfield, pulled out a gun, and shot himself in the head. The last story was about an English teacher who showed her class *Star Trek* videos every day for five weeks before disappearing without a trace. She was last seen wandering through the half-empty Wood County Mall in full Klingon regalia. It was like a sick postmodern version of *Winesberg, Ohio* without the pastoralism, without hope. They said goodbye. Joe hung up without an ounce of homesickness.

It was 3:00 P.M. and Joe had nothing to do. He put some Greg Osby on his stereo, walked over to his nightstand and grabbed a half-smoked joint and a book of matches out of the top drawer. Joe lit the joint, took two deep hits, smelled the thick sweet smell, and watched the smoke fill the air. Osby's jazz was one long song with no breaks—he drifted in and out of melodies separated by periods of prolonged dissonance. Joe lost himself in it. He struggled through a series of atonal notes until he hit a deep vein of melodic saxophone. It pulsed in steps like a heartbeat rising toward ecstasy. The phone rang and his machine took it. It was the credit card company hounding him for a late payment. Joe sighed, put the matches and the roach into his pocket, turned off his stereo, and walked out the door of his studio.

The hallway smelled like strong perfume, burned hot dogs, and his pot smoke. There was nobody there but he could hear muffled voices behind doors, a peal of laughter, and the sound of a TV game show. The late afternoon sunlight glowed around the front door, lending it an aura of gentleness. Joe walked out onto Fifth, crossed over at Hawthorne, and kept going until he hit Fourth Avenue. He decided to drift downtown. At Grape Street he stopped to look at the huge Moreton Bay Fig alongside the parking lot that used to be the historic Florence Hotel. Joe tried to imagine what the grand old Victorian would have looked like. Did a man wander past this spot to ponder this tree a hundred years ago and wonder what it might look like now? How many people had idled here, thinking of love or death in the midst of an inconsequential day? The ghosts of the past haunt us, Joe thought, despite our efforts to exorcise them. He moved on past medical offices, a take-out chicken place, two bland hotels, and a rooming house.

Past Elm he came upon the red brick gothic First Presbyterian Church. The stained-glass windows were covered with Plexiglas, and a gathering of homeless men lingered on the steps in front taking in the muted sound of the music trickling out of the church. Joe walked past them and into the church to listen to the organist practice. He caught the last few seconds of what sounded like Bach and followed the final dying note as it rose toward the arched ceiling. He watched the organist sit in the naked silence for a moment. If there was a God, it lived inside that silence, Joe thought. The organist turned and nodded to him across the empty pews. Joe said, "Beautiful," and left him to his solitude.

He crossed Date Street where Olmsted had envisioned a promenade from the harbor to the park, walked over the freeway bridge where the growing flow of pre-rush-hour traffic hummed beneath him. Joe passed a law school and, in the midst of the crosswalk at Cedar Street, glanced toward the harbor. His eyes were drawn to a square of glistening silver framed by the main entrance to the Art Deco County Administration Building. It was like a door to a dream of pure light, so bright it hurt his eyes. A black Jeep honked, startling Joe out of his reverie and out of the middle of the street. He ambled by Catholic Charities and the cream colored Moorish tower of Saint Joseph's Cathedral with the red sun just above it. There were steel grates on the windows. It was as if they were afraid someone would steal God.

Joe moved on, looked up at the open windows in the downtrodden Centre City Apartments where he saw an old woman sitting in shadows and a shirtless man with a hard face and a tattooed chest leaning out of a window smoking a cigarette, staring down at the parking lot. As he passed the lobby, he glanced in at the TV playing to an empty room as the desk clerk read a paperback novel. There was an angry, desperate-looking woman cursing into the payphone outside the adjoining liquor store. Joe walked by another parking lot, the prison-like family court building, a live/work space with a Victorian front, the old cinderblock and iron Arts and Crafts Richard Requa building, and the Dianetics Foundation to Ash Street. At Ash, Joe was struck by the way the Imperial, Union, Wells Fargo, and Bank of America towers loomed, dwarfing the old HBJ building and casting long shadows on the street. They were graceless structures with no redeeming value, but their placement and size announced their dominance. We are your faceless masters, they said. Joe thought of Allen Ginsberg roaming the streets of San Francisco on peyote, ranting at the Saint Francis Hotel. He smiled and strolled by a hair salon in an old bank lobby, a concert venue that had also been a bank. Moloch, he thought, Moloch destroyer of men.

At B Street, Joe looked up at the fading ad painted in red, green, white, and brown on the brick side of the vacant California Theatre: "San Diego's 'In Spot' on the corner of 4th and C." He walked by the boarded up window of what used to be a hot dog stand, remembered the smell of Polish sausages on the grill, the row of customers sitting at stools, resting their forearms on the greasy counter.

The front entrance to the theater was boarded up as well, plastered with dozens of the same movie poster featuring an ironic retro-seventies, leggy platinum blond in hot pants, bent over a red Camaro, again and again. Someone had put stickers over several of the posters—sketches of the dead wrestler Andre the Giant's face with the caption "OBEY." Joe stopped and read the flyer entitled "Giant Manifesto" that someone had glued up next to one of the Andres: *"The Andre the Giant sticker attempts to stimulate curiosity and bring people to question both the sticker and their relationship with their surroundings. Because people are not used to seeing advertisements or propaganda for which the product or motive is not obvious, frequent and novel encounters with the sticker provoke thought and possible frustration, nevertheless revitalizing the viewer's perception and attention to detail. The sticker has no meaning but exists only to cause people to react, to contemplate and search for meaning in the sticker."* Joe saw little difference between the ad and the sticker. He noticed that passersby were looking at him as if he were insane. Who reads walls? He turned to go and glanced across the street at the Cubist-inspired mural on the side of the trendy live/work lofts above Mrs. Field's Cookies.

Joe crossed C Street and noticed that the foot traffic was thicker. Office people were steadily flowing out of their cubicles to briefly join the homeless, the tourists, and the hotel dwellers. Joe passed by a man in a black Armani suit who embodied everything he hated—dark glasses, little gold earring, cell phone, neatly trimmed hair, gym-fit body, own-the-world walk. Something about him suggested the Internet, image management, heartless innovation, and a massive stock portfolio. If you ate his heart you would shit disdain, Joe thought. He wondered for a moment how he could judge so quickly on the basis of appearance until he heard the man say "NASDAQ" into his phone. Joe watched a group of women in pantsuits walk by with cagey eyes and careful postures. A couple in Sea World shirts were speaking French. After them followed a man in army fatigues with long hair and a stars and stripes headband, swinging a stick in the air as he said, "dream flowers," to no one in particular. Joe took it all in and headed into the lounge in the U.S. Grant Hotel.

It was dark inside and Joe blinked until he could see the parquet floor, the oak paneling by the bookshelves, and the portrait of U.S. Grant above the fireplace and the luxuriant pool table. Joe decided to have a drink. He sat down at a table by the window and the proper-looking waitress came by to take his order—a vodka soda. She walked over to the bar and Joe watched her. She looked fragile, serious, but kind. There was an elderly man in a dirty yellow suit at the bar, eating all the bowls of cocktail peanuts. He ordered a glass of water and she brought it to him. The old man ran out of peanuts at the bar and moved to an empty table with a full bowl. After he finished, he relocated to a booth by the far wall to eat some pretzels. The bartender walked over and asked him to leave. Joe noticed the waitress looking on sadly, biting her lower lip. She brought Joe his drink. He paid and looked across the street at the lobby of the Plaza Hotel. There were people sitting in chairs watching traffic, glancing over at the lounge, waiting for no one, nothing. Somebody walked out of the lobby and into China King next door. The old man in the dirty yellow suit walked into the lobby of the Plaza. Joe sipped his drink, stared at the blue-and-white-checkered awning above the door of the Greek restaurant on the other side of the Plaza. The dentist's office was closed, as was Maria's Mexican food. Joe savored the tired, lonely block bathed in darkening shadows.

He finished his drink, left a dollar tip, and walked to the hotel lobby through the lounge by the long line of booths against the oak walls with delicate fabric inlays. He strolled under a crystal chandelier and by a pair of antique wooden chairs to the men's room. He peed in a stall and took a quick hit off what remained of the roach, leaving the smoke in the air behind him as he left. Back in the lobby, Joe aimlessly wandered past oil paintings in ornately carved gilt frames—a dark forest scene, a dreamy pastoral river. He sat down in a chair in the corner and stared up at the elaborate gold and green moldings that bordered the ceiling. His eyes slid down the marble columns to the green carpet decorated with brown and tan medallions with flowers at their centers. There was oak around the doorways, rich red carpet on the stairs, a cream and gold fili-greed iron railing on the walkway on the second floor. Joe thought of Emma Goldman in this lobby. She had wanted to address a lynch mob from an upstairs window. Brave, sweet Emma in the pompous U.S. Grant. Her ghost was with him here, thumbing her nose at the dot.com nouveau riche. Joe felt a tap on his shoulder. A security guard was asking him to leave.

Out on Broadway, Joe gazed across the street at the Irving Gill fountain in Horton Plaza Park, the water spouting up toward the Moorish copper cap before sprinkling back down the Doric col-umns into the octagonal pool. It was beautiful in the midst of the palm trees and potted plants behind chains. The grotesquely huge lizard on the Planet Hollywood sign, however, made the whole square absurd. Joe watched people carrying bags out of the mall as he crossed the street and made his way down Fourth, past the small park. He saw a group of Germans in beachwear sitting on backpacks alongside the wall of the mall looking in *Let's Go California,* teenagers with skateboards, preoccupied shoppers, happy-hour seekers, and tired mall workers at the bus stop. Joe looked at people's feet—sandals, leather loafers with tassels, high heels, Con-verse sneakers, dirty boots, Doc Martins, running shoes, platforms, flip flops, Birkenstocks, pumps, and filthy bare feet. He looked up across the street at the tops of the turn of the century buildings in the Gaslamp, his eyes exploring the arched windows, elaborate moldings, peaked roofs, and Victorian flourishes. Joe imagined a street above the street, ramps connecting rooftops, winding purposelessly throughout the city, trading only in the commerce of wonder and sky. Above the jewelry store and the lobster restaurant, the new, Joe thought. He smiled and kept going.

As he walked on, Joe glanced up at the domed top of the Balboa Theatre, decorated with blue and yellow mosaic tile and round portholes. The old Romanesque structure had been a vaudeville place and a movie palace in the 1920s. He stopped and read a sign on the wall that displayed a picture of the lobby with its fine woodwork and elaborately sculpted waterfalls. Some vaudeville acts here had featured live elephants. Joe strolled on, past the window display on San Diego's history. He stopped and read a sign about how Alonzo Horton bought the site of the city for two hundred and sixty-five dollars and built the Horton House where the U.S. Grant stands today. Boost it and they will come, Joe thought. The next sign was about the now-dead Chinatown and the red light district, the Stingaree. Joe had read about the brothels and opium dens. Ignored by the police, this area was riddled with maze-like passageways, hidden rooms, and secret chambers. There was a city beneath the city, subterranean spaces waiting. Joe dreamed of a labyrinth made for drifting. The architecture of his desire would open the maze beneath the city, creating a park beneath the streets comprised of passageways bathed in dim red light that occasionally opened to pool chambers, rooms filled with music of all kinds, snug little bars and opium dens, hidden libraries and free art galleries, rooms of light and color, beds for unashamed sex, spaces of pure silence, doors into mystery. A fat man in an ugly brown suit stopped next to Joe to read the same sign. He looked at him, smiled and said, "It was more fun then." Joe smiled back and nodded.

The next sign was about Little Italy and the tuna industry. Joe looked at a picture of Italian and Japanese fishermen wearing straw and felt fedoras, hauling in tuna with huge poles. There were also photographs of the El Cortez being built during the Depression, the "nudist beach" at the 1935 Exposition, and the Douglass Hotel and Creole Palace nightclub. Joe studied a black-and-white photo of dancing girls and jazz players by the entrance to the Creole Palace, the girls kneeling in front smiling, the men standing behind them, holding saxophones and clarinets next to a sign that said "Harlem of the West." The final section was entitled "Boomtown's Still Boomin'" and was dedicated to hyping redevelopment and tourism. Joe read about the "visionary plan" for the ballpark, the "music village," the "urban art trail." The city was changing existing Fifth Avenue buildings into "a dynamic entertainment complex," the sign said. There would be "stylish nightclubs, exciting gourmet restaurants, upscale lofts, and expanded parking." The city was reinventing itself—again. He looked across the street at the Hard Rock Cafe in what used to be the Golden Lion and something else before that. He could see Victorian cupolas and the Hotel Saint James rising beyond them on Sixth Avenue. Is history still history, Joe wondered, when it becomes a mere backdrop?

Joe continued down Fourth Avenue past a taco shop, the F Street Bookstore, a cigar cafe, and two expensive Italian restaurants. He glanced across the street at the Moon Cafe and KD's Donuts, funky remnants of the old downtown. The juxtaposition of these places with the sea of newness that surrounded them lent them the air of museum pieces, places where affluent diners and bar goers could glance in at gritty pockets of poverty. Perhaps they should pay the grizzled men at the counters, Joe thought, like characters at Disneyland. He remembered the fallen downtown with all the sailors, strip joints, diners, arcades, pawn shops, and porn theaters and was filled with a strange nostalgia for urban decay. Joe walked by the Metro Market and Wash, hit the Golden West Hotel, and decided to walk through the lobby. The Golden West was built in 1913 but had none of the pretense of the U.S. Grant. People lived here. Joe looked down at the red Persianesque carpet and over at the worn

Arts and Crafts straight-back chairs. One of them was occupied by a man with wild green eyes and bushy black hair who sat rocking, repeating "I got tired of making babies and dancing like Fred Astaire," over and over again. There was a fading painting of Torrey Pines on the peach wall above his head. It looked like a picture postcard from the twenties. Joe came to the ancient wooden front desk with grated windows, looked up at the cubbyholes for the keys and the mail, the "thank you come again" sign. To the right of the desk was a group of hotel residents sitting in big, battered rocking chairs staring at the huge TV screen. "America's Most Wanted" was on. To the left, the old switchboard was on display next to the vending machines and the antique phone booths. Joe looked down and noticed that the carpet had given way to black and white ceramic tile.

"Need a room?" said a voice from behind the desk.

"No thanks," said Joe "I'm just looking."

"Take your time," the voice said.

Joe glanced back over at the people watching TV: an old woman in a red and black polka-dot dress; two men in U.S.S. Constitution hats; a young girl with an old face, rocking slowly, not watching the show. A group of tourists, young women speaking Italian, came down the stairs. The TV crowd didn't look at them. Joe saw that one of the girls was stunningly beautiful. He stared at her luxuriant black hair, perfect olive skin, and full, sensuous figure barely contained by a little blue sundress. She stared back at him with bright piercing eyes, smiled broadly, laughed with her friends, and kept walking. Joe felt aroused and embarrassed, let them pass for a moment, and headed back through the lobby to Fourth Avenue. "I used to make babies and dance like Fred Astaire," said the man on the chair by the door.

As he crossed G Street, Joe walked by an ugly apartment tower, the Rock Bottom Brewery, a cheese shop, and Hooters to Market

72

Street. He passed an antiques store, Café Bassan, Café Sévilla, a new gourmet restaurant where the pie factory used to be, a sushi place, an electrolysis studio, and the Gaslamp Quarter Hotel. There was a new restaurant going into the Ah Quin Building. Ah Quin had been the "mayor of Chinatown" in the 1930s. His house was Spanish Colonial Revival style. Joe glanced over at the canary yellow Davis House museum, turned right on Island by the Horton Grand Hotel, built in the 1880s on another site and reassembled here one-hundred years later. He glanced in the at the lounge, thought about a drink, changed his mind, kept going to Third Avenue, and turned left down the last remaining block of Chinatown. The Quong building used to be a brothel and an opium den and was now a chic Mexican café. Joe stopped and looked at Quin Produce across the street as a pedicab rolled by carrying two midwestern tourists in Green Bay Packers T-shirts listening to a canned litany of sanitized local history. He strolled past the Chinese Historical Building and read a sign that told him it was built by a cousin of Irving Gill's.

Joe was struck by the fact that he was walking through a calculated pastiche, looking for unplanned ruptures that let in the unexpected. He had hit a dry spell. He tried to stop thinking, let it go. Joe came to J Street, turned left and ambled by a parking lot. He crossed Fourth and glanced over at a billiards hall built to look old, a "real" old blue, yellow, and burgundy Victorian, Fifth Avenue lined with SUVs, a wine bank, an antique store, and a warehouse that was now apartments. At Sixth and J, Joe noticed a mural painted on the side of a citrus warehouse—two huge staring eyes in pastel gold and turquoise with big black pupils under a single thick brow. Who is watching? he wondered. There were more antiques places, live/work lofts, and storage units. At Seventh, he turned right, passed Dizzy's jazz club, the Clarion Hotel, and more warehouses until he crossed K Street and saw the Western Metal Supply Company, the site of the new ballpark. At Seventh and K, Joe stopped and looked over at the frame of the new convention center, the shipyards and the Coronado bridge beyond it. In front of him was the huge empty expanse that used to be the warehouse district. It was fenced off. They had annihilated a piece of the city and were starting over. He tried to imagine the space of the city a hundred years hence. Joe retraced his steps. At the corner of Seventh and J, he noticed another pair of eyes staring over the top of a warehouse. Who was watching? What was it that connected him with the past and left his trace for the future? Who was watching? He didn't know.

At Fifth, Joe turned right and walked past the Island Hotel and a Thai place that used to be the oldest Chinese restaurant in the city. He remembered the sawdust on the floor and the boxing posters from the thirties on the walls over the booths in the old Chinese place. He crossed the street and made a brief detour on Island to look at the Callan Hotel. It had been a Japanese business before it was stolen during the days of internment. There was a woman on the steps outside smoking a cigarette. Joe nodded to her as he looked up toward the roof of the building.

"You a student or something?" asked the woman before taking another drag off her cigarette. Her two front teeth were missing and her cheeks were sunken, but she had lively brown eyes.

"No, a teacher actually." Joe said a little awkwardly. "I'm just interested in buildings, history."

"Well, there's a lot of history in there," she said gesturing back towards the door with a gruff laugh. "History you don't want to know." She lit another cigarette and took a deep drag.

"You have a good evening," Joe said as he turned back toward Fifth Avenue.

"You too, sweetheart," she said earnestly, "You too."

Joe passed the Blarney Stone, an art gallery, more historic site plaques, yuppie party bars, a reconstruction of an Irish pub, a cigar bar, a sushi place, and another gourmet restaurant until he hit

Market Street. While he waited at the light, he turned around and looked in the window of the wig shop on the corner. There were ridiculous fuzzy blue, red, and fluorescent yellow wigs on styrofoam heads with long necks, painted eyes, and cheap sunglasses. It was wonderfully absurd. Joe crossed Market and the weeknight crowd thickened. He passed by a group of sharply dressed Mexican teenagers on nervous first dates, some white skate punks with pink and purple hair, a pack of drunken office people, an ancient man with a gaunt, Creole face in a cowboy hat carrying a guitar case, two sailors in full uniform, people speaking a language he couldn't place, two hipsters with nose rings, one in a bowling shirt, the other in a T-shirt that said, "Jesus is coming soon, look busy."

A Japanese tourist was standing in the middle of the street taking a picture of the gold-capped cones and ornate Victorian decorations on the top of the Yuma Building. Joe glanced across the street at a family sitting at a table in the fancy new retro-fifties soda fountain that used to be the Casino Theatre. He remembered seeing dollar movies there, reveling in the eccentric crowd of homeless people, sailors, prostitutes, security guards and janitors sleeping before the nightshift, whole families, seniors, vice cops, and drug dealers. It had been the kind of place where people talked back to the screen. Before that, it had been a porno theater, before that, a respectable movie palace. Joe looked over at the Urban Outfitters that had been the Aztec Theater, back across the street at the Greystone Steakhouse that used to be the Bijou. He missed the gritty, chaotic democracy of the old dollar theaters. Anything might happen there, and frequently did. He remembered seeing a woman do calisthenics in the aisle during a horror film at the Bijou and watching a man stand up in the middle of *Mississippi Burning* at the Casino and deliver a political speech. They were just ghosts now, though, fading memories. There wasn't any room left for the cheap theaters or the people who went there. Everything had to be upscale, big money. He hated much of the gentrified downtown, but he realized that many of the old things he loved had started in the same way as these new places. The bright lights and the hype brought out the crowd and Joe refused to give up on the crowd. Even in the midst of the most calculated theme park zone, he thought, was the potential for a newness that superseded commercial intent. You have to learn to be surprised by the place you know, Joe thought, to find wonder and poetry in the street outside your door, to unlock the residual dream in the streets. He bumped into a light post and told himself to stop thinking.

As he crossed G Street, Joe noticed that the avenue was even busier. He made his way slowly through the throng, glanced over at the long row of people waiting in line by the fake Victorian front of the new movie palace, passed by several Italian restaurants, smelling garlic, hearing the murmur of a dozen conversations. He weaved in and out of clusters of people waiting in lines or stopping to talk, ambled by Lee's Cafe, a pawn shop, Bella Luna, Little Joe's, Lulu's Boutique, and the Bitter End, a fancy martini bar that used to be the Orient, a sailor joint with huge fish tanks. Joe stopped for a moment and stood on the corner, losing himself in the river of faces. A gorgeous black couple kissed gleefully as they crossed the street next to a preoccupied waiter on his way to work. There was despair in the eyes of a man in rumpled blue suit and joy on the face of a laughing secretary, playfully holding hands with a friend.

For a moment, Joe imagined he could read the whole of people's lives in their faces and know impossible secrets. He glanced at a lovely woman in a long black evening dress and felt that tomorrow might be her last day. Joe laughed at his fancy, while still marveling at the awesome mystery of this random collection of human consciousnesses, thrown together here on this street at this precise moment in time by chance. He watched the woman in the evening gown stop to speak with a man sitting on the sidewalk with a cup.

What was there between them? Between everyone? A kid with long cornrows in a Forty-niners jersey strolled by singing only to himself. The doorman stared lustfully at a woman in a very short red skirt. People touched each other as they zigzagged through the crowd. It was a warm night and the street was teeming with desire. All of us, Joe thought, are pregnant with death; all of us want our beings to sing in the time that we have. A little boy bumped into his leg and was dragged away quickly by his mother. Joe watched people watching other people as they made their way through the crowd. He gazed at people sipping wine in a restaurant patio and watched the way men and women looked at each other. At the most basic level, we want to eat, fuck, and sing, Joe thought. We yearn and hope. And for that moment, he felt a kind of undifferentiated connection to people that he knew would never last.

Joe crossed F Street and looked up at the Keating Building, built in 1890, the office of the cheesy TV detectives in *Simon and Simon*. The sound of a tenor saxophone was echoing out of Croce's. Joe stopped outside the entrance, leaned on a light post, and glanced up at the Nesmith-Creely Building across the street, its red-brick frame topped with marvelous spires. Next to it was a building with even more elaborate stonework, brown, green, white, and gold detailed woodwork, and two wondrous towers. It was twilight and the dying violet sky was blending with the glow from the street, giving the scene a feeling of magic. The saxophone rose and fell. Joe noticed that a homeless man was standing next to him looking up as well. Several other people stopped to glance up with them. "What's up there?" said a man gruffly to his wife who'd stopped to look because others had. "Wonder," Joe said, before moving on out of the thick of the crowd, past one of the last peep shows, San Diego Hardware, Western Hat Works, Far East Imports, a couple of cheap restaurants, a sports shoes outlet, Lee's Menswear, an expensive new resort hotel, the Art Deco Universal Boot Shop, a check cashing place,

Master Tattoo "since 1949," Subway, and Louisiana Fried Chicken. By the time he hit Broadway, the streets were nearly empty. There was vomit mixed with blood on the sidewalk. Joe looked at the bus stop a few feet away. A man was lying face down under the bench. Joe walked over to him. It was Bob Anderson. He took the last five dollars out of his pocket, leaned over, and gently stuffed the money into Bob's dirty jacket, taking care not to wake him. He didn't stir. Joe stood up and walked over to the corner to wait at the red light. It was dark now and his feet hurt badly.

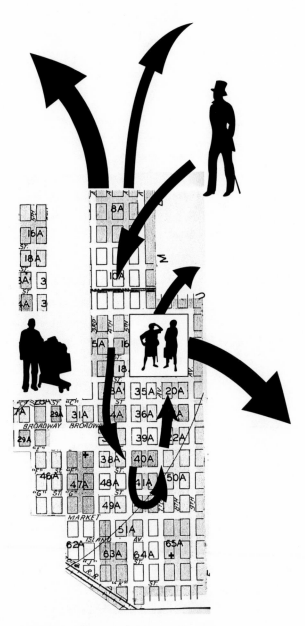

Psychogeographic map of the Gaslamp District
San Diego, California.

14   Chuck woke up to the sound of a car alarm going off down on the street below his room at the Golden West Hotel. He rolled over on his side and stared at the newspaper he had dropped on the floor before falling asleep. It was folded over to page fourteen and the headline, "Government Says National Sacrifice Zones Will Never Be Salvaged." Whatever, Chuck thought. He sat up slowly, groaned, and rubbed his eyes until he saw a strange, checkered pattern of light behind his lids. When he opened them there was the blank white wall and his dirty gray pants were on the back of the chair. A car horn blared outside. Chuck grabbed a cigarette out of the pack on the nightstand and lit it with a cheap purple lighter. He took a drag, blew it out, stood up, pulled on his pants, and grabbed a plain white T-shirt out of the top drawer of the dresser. He left the shade down, walked over to the sink and splashed some water on his rugged, pockmarked face. He stared at some old scars and brushed back his short, spiky white hair with his hands. Old and ugly, he thought.

After wiping his face dry with a musty hand towel, Chuck tossed it on top of the dresser and glanced back in the mirror at the skull and cross bones tattooed on his meaty forearm. He was a big, hulking man, still strong for sixty. Nobody got in his way on the street. Chuck sat back down on the bed and put on his scuffed black leather shoes. He was hungry. He got up and walked out of his room, through the dim hallway to the stairs. As he made his way down, Chuck looked at the people sitting in rockers, watching TV. Nobody he cared about. Some guy was nosing around the lobby like the place was a museum. Stupid asshole, Chuck thought. He felt like walking over and laying him out just for the hell of it. In the old days, he would have. Now, he just muttered to himself and walked by the idiot babbling about Fred Astaire in the chair by the door. "Fuck you and Fred Astaire," he growled at the man.

Chuck walked across the middle of Fourth Avenue towards the Moon Café and a woman in a huge truck honked at him when she had to stop to let him pass. He turned around, flipped her off, and glared at her with notable intensity. She drove around him in a huff. "Bitch," Chuck muttered to himself. In the Moon Café, he sat down next to a guy he used to drink with in the Naha before it closed.

"Hey, Arnie," Chuck said as he slapped him on the back.

"How's it hangin'?" Arnie replied.

"All the way down my left pants leg," Chuck said with a laugh. The middle-aged Korean woman behind the counter looked at them coolly and walked over to take their orders—two $1.99 breakfast specials and fifty-cent coffees. She wiped down the counter with a wet dishrag but the grease was so thick it still stuck to Chuck's forearms. "I could write my name in this shit," he grumbled to Arnie. Arnie laughed and nodded.

"You remember Big Jack from the Naha?" Arnie asked.

"Sure," said Chuck.

"He died over in the Maryland last week."

"What of?" asked Chuck.

"Don't know, but I heard it took a couple of days until anybody missed him. He was stiff as a board when they found him. Nobody knew who to call."

"Well, I guess somebody's got to give the firemen a reason to stand around and scratch their asses. You ever see how many guys show up just to drag off a corpse?" Chuck said.

"It's like a goddamned block party," Arnie agreed. The food came. They both ate slowly and silently, nursing the runny eggs and charred bacon, sipping the weak, watery coffee. Chuck glanced out the window at a group of pretty young Italian girls in short skirts. One of them dropped something and bent over to pick it up. Chuck felt the blood flowing down below. "I wouldn't mind that," he said as he nudged Arnie.

"Keep dreamin', you old fuck," Arnie said. They laughed and Arnie put down his fork and wiped his plate clean with a piece of dry toast.

"Maybe I'll just jump off the bridge before they have to carry me out past a crowd of strangers," Arnie said.

"Shut the fuck up," said Chuck, "You'll die wanking off in bed and they'll put a picture of your rigor mortis on the front page." Arnie laughed, said goodbye gruffly, left three dollars on the counter, and walked out the door. Chuck finished his coffee and looked over at the woman behind the counter.

"What do you say?" he offered.

"Nothing to you," she said, smiling with cruel pleasure. Chuck smirked, blew her a mock kiss, left two dollars and fifty cents on the counter, and walked out onto Fourth Avenue. Some teenagers in nice new clothes sitting on the sidewalk outside a fancy restaurant asked him for change.

"You're kidding me, right?" Chuck snarled. He thought back to the days when this whole street was full of strip bars, porn theaters, and nickel-and-dime places. Today you couldn't get a whore without a credit card and the yellow pages. Once he'd left the Navy, he'd worked as a bartender, a bouncer, a security guard, a hotel desk clerk, and a cashier at a peep show. Now he was just taking checks and squeezing by. Nobody wanted an ugly decrepit geezer to check IDs at the door. Chuck walked by the Hard Rock Café and spit on the sidewalk in front of the door. He crossed the street and lumbered by the mall. The suits and shoppers were out in full force. The pretty young girls with bags didn't look at him and the suits stepped out of his way. It was all too goddamned clean and shiny.

He felt like hitting someone. Chuck crossed Broadway and walked past the doorman outside the U.S. Grant. How could he wear that cute little uniform? Chuck shook his head in disgust, hit Third Avenue, and made his way by an office complex, Second Avenue, another office complex, First Avenue, the Greyhound Bus terminal, a 99 Cent Store, a cheap deli and mini mart, and a barber shop before he came to the Piccadilly Bar, the last outpost on the last remaining block of the old West Broadway.

"Hey, Chuck," the bartender said.

"Hey, Larry," Chuck said, "How 'bout a draft?" Larry poured one, and Chuck paid just as Scottie strolled in the front door. He was wearing an Airborne hat, dark sunglasses, an Army surplus jacket, and camo pants. He walked up to some kids sitting with backpacks, sipping Cokes. They were probably waiting for a bus. Scottie started telling them tall tales about Vietnam and asked the kids to buy him a beer. They did. Chuck waited until the beer had been paid for and yelled, "The only war Scottie ever fought in was with his ex-wife!"

"Fuck you, Chuck!" Scottie yelled.

"Not for all the tea in China!" Chuck shot back. Scottie rushed over to the bar and knocked over Chuck's beer. Chuck stood up and flattened him with one punch. Scottie stayed on his back, mumbling obscenities.

"Take a walk, Chuck," Larry said firmly.

"No problem, Larry," Chuck agreed. He got up, winked at the kids in the corner, and walked out the door, down towards the harbor past the new courthouse, the YMCA, and a huge new office tower. Chuck tried to remember where Cindy's Topless A-Go-Go had been. When he had been a bouncer there, the girls danced on a tiny stage behind the bar where Little Gus, in a starched white shirt with a black bow tie, was serving up drinks. After work, Chuck would go over to Downtown Johnny's diner and order a burger or a grilled cheese sandwich. You could sit there for hours, as long as you kept buying coffee. He remembered talking all night there with one of the girls from Cindy's and walking with her out into the dawn with a sense of invincibility. "We'll never die," he'd said to her with mock bravado. She had laughed and kissed him lingeringly, passionately. He couldn't remember what had happened to her, sweet thing, and he wasn't sure where any of the old places had been.

Chuck moved on, past the new tower, over the trolley tracks by Santa Fe Station. Sometimes he liked to buy a cup of coffee there, read the paper, and watch the people come and go. Not today though, he didn't feel like it. Chuck kept walking all the way to the harbor, turned right, and trudged by the tourist ships, Anthony's Fish Grotto, and the Star of India. He ignored all the happy, tan people. There weren't any fishing boats left anymore. He sat down by the water and let the breeze gently blow on his face. The sun was bright and hot and the water was deep, deep blue. Chuck felt he was at the end of the world somehow, out of gas. Sometimes he thought he might want to say something, express something, utter a dying croak. There were no words though. And what did he have to say anyway? Chuck thought about jumping in, sinking down, and never coming back up.

15

Rosie finished clipping the bright red roses in the tiny patch of garden outside her little green cottage on Fir street, took off her gloves, and walked up the front steps into the living room to check her messages. Angie wanted to know if she would help set up the church picnic next Sunday and her daughter had to switch their shopping day from today to tomorrow. Michael had an earache, poor baby. That left today open. Rosie looked up at the picture of her husband, long dead, on the mantle. It was her favorite shot of him, standing bare-chested, tan, and handsome on the deck of his old tuna boat. The muscles rippled on his arms as he leaned on the railing and his big brown eyes were full of pride. His smile was playful, a little sneaky looking, that Tony. Those days were long gone though. Rosie smiled to herself and walked into the kitchen to wash her hands. She needed some things for dinner with the grandchildren this Saturday. Rosie headed back into the living room and looked in the mirror to straighten her thick gray hair. Her face was full of kind wrinkles, but she had color in her cheeks and smart, lively eyes. Not bad for an old girl, she thought. Rosie grabbed her purse off the wingback chair by the door and walked up to India Street to buy some prosciutto. She walked past Filippi's to Italian Village where the prosciutto was the cheapest. They should call it Mexican Village, she thought. She couldn't remember the last time she'd seen an Italian behind the counter. They were good to her though. Hard workers, family people. She got the meat from a nice looking boy, very polite, and walked back out onto the sidewalk. She stopped as her eyes adjusted to the glare and glanced down the street toward La Pensione, where the tourists stayed, and some fancy new condos. They were fixing the place up. It was nicer now. Not much of the old neighborhood left though. The freeway had almost killed it. Very Little Italy, she thought.

Rosie headed back to her house, put the prosciutto in the fridge and decided it was too nice a day to stay inside. She found her sunglasses on the table by the door and walked back out to Kettner, past a car dealership, to Grape Street. It was a good day to be by the water. Rosie ambled down to the harbor and stopped for a moment to look at it. The midday sun was dancing gold on the water, and the white sails of ships beckoned. She took a deep breath of salty air. Tony had always loved that smell. Almost all the fishing boats were gone now, though, and so was the cannery were she had worked as a young woman. Down the harbor a ways past Seaport Village it had been. Seaport Village was a nice mall, she thought. It didn't smell like fish guts. Rosie walked past some cute little boys fishing near the pier and a mean-looking guy sitting by the edge of the water, staring down at it sullenly. She strolled by the U.S.S. Berkeley Museum and the Star of India. She liked watching all the tourists walking around, taking pictures of everything. There was a long line of people standing outside Anthony's Fish Grotto, and Rosie noticed a little girl staring up at her with big blue eyes. "Hello, beautiful," she said and smiled. The girl's parents smiled back at her, and Rosie kept going towards the cruise ship terminal, looking up at the massive white boat, big as a street block, looming above the dock. She wondered what a cruise was like—if there was dancing in the moonlight and champagne. Past the terminal, she walked by a man in a wheelchair with a sign that said, "Homeless veteran, please help." Rosie took a quarter out of her purse and dropped it into the cup in his lap. "God bless you," he said.

A pack of pedicabs was waiting by the harbor cruises and one of the boys asked Rosie if she wanted a ride. She briefly thought of asking one of the strong young men to take her up the big hill at Laurel Street to the park. She would sit in the back and yell: "faster, honey, faster." Rosie said, "No, thank you," and giggled to herself a little as she got in line to buy a ticket for the Coronado Ferry. She paid three dollars for a round trip ticket and strolled over to the boat. Rosie walked down the plank to the dock, politely refused the souvenir picture, and followed a man carrying a mountain bike on board. She climbed the steps and got a nice seat in the sun on the top deck. She sat down and watched the people come aboard. A big family with four little ones, each one carrying a can of soda, the smallest child's hand almost too small to hold the can. Then there were young couples holding hands, some nervously, some comfortably. Rosie watched them and thought she could guess who would marry and who would not. There were people speaking Japanese, Spanish, and German, more people with bikes, people in fancy running outfits. It was like everyone was training for the Olympics nowadays.

The last passenger came aboard and the boat pulled away from the dock slowly. The wind picked up, and the sun was warm on Rosie's face. She looked over at a handsome couple kissing in front of her. The boy had his shirt off and his muscles rippled as he put his arm behind the girl. Rosie remembered the times Tony would take her out to the empty boat to watch the sunset. They would drink wine, laugh, and make love in the warm summer air. Rosie looked up at a sea gull flying high in the blue sky above the boat, listened to the children laughing behind her. This Saturday, she would look at her grandson Michael's face and see Tony. This was the connection between them, God's way of reminding her. Rosie smiled at the mother of the four children as she ran over to keep her little girl from getting too close to the railing. Suddenly she was filled with a feeling of great love. It was all connected, she thought. This was a good life. Rosie closed her eyes, breathed in the sea air, and felt the boat gently riding on the deep water.

16 *From the 1880s on, the desperate came to San Diego, filling the rooms of the Florence Hotel, the Kneipp Sanitarium, Los Banos, the Saint Helena and Saint James, the Horton House, the Agnew, the Arlington, and the Hotel Del Coronado. The pallid tourists arrived from the East with consumption, asthma, rheumatism, and a host of other acute maladies. If the hydrotherapy, magnetizers, sitz baths, and salt glows did not work, maybe the sun would. With the sun came hope. Perhaps the newcomers had read John Bower's pamphlet "San Diego as a Summer Resort for Pleasure Seekers and Invalids" or the article by Dr. Peter Remondino in the* San Diego Advertiser *where he crowed that: "The United States has a small section away in its southwestern corner, which will give to a man a life of ease, comfort, luxury, and besides allow him at the same time to accumulate wealth to any amount. If you have any doubt about this just look at the early Americans who came here in the period following the annexation of California. They are endowed with Falstaffian paunches, Bonifacial noses and Teutonic complexions of roses; never sick; with digestions to be envied by the ostrich or alligator; lungs like a blacksmith's bellows and hearts as tough as that of a turtle. Their muscles are firm and their frames sturdy and their bank accounts are unlimited, their main occupation being the clipping off of coupons from their stores of bonds. There is evident proof of the physical and financial effects of our climate which cannot be gainsaid." It was here, under the sunny blue sky by the Pacific that the Anglo Saxon stock, made sickly by social woes and the damp weather*

of the East could renew and reinvent itself. But, when this Social Dar-
winist panacea proved futile, the Pacific turned into a hostile void,
the "jumping off place" as Edmund Wilson noted in the 1930s, com-
menting on the rising numbers of suicides, as the exuberance of sun-
light gave way to disease, poverty, emptiness, and death.

PACIFIC BEACH

there was a kind of wonderful, stupid, oversexed joy oozing out of the crowd

17

Joe woke up to the sound of the phone ringing. He let the machine pick up. It was his mother's voice, strained and full of tears, "Joe this is Mom, please give me a call immediately." He jumped out of bed and grabbed the phone. "What's the matter Mom?" he asked.

"Your father passed away."

"When?"

"Last night. He had a heart attack and died before they could get him to the hospital."

"I'm sorry, Mom. How are you?"

"It hasn't sunk in yet," she said numbly. "It doesn't feel real."

"Is there anything I can do?"

"No, Joe, there isn't. I know you two didn't get along, but I just thought you should know. "

"I'm sorry, Mom."

"It's not your fault, Joe. I loved your father, but he was a hard man."

"What are you going to do?"

"His brothers are taking care of the details. I haven't thought beyond that. Can you come back for the service, Joe?"

"I don't know, Mom," he said tightly. "The money's short."

"You do what you can, dear. Listen, I have to go."

"I love you, Mom," he said sadly.

"I know, honey. I love you too."

Joe hung up and stood for a while, letting it sink in. He hadn't spoken to his father in three years, not since he had told him he was a coward for hitting his mother, not since he'd told her to leave and she didn't. Now he was gone, and Joe's anger turned to numbness as he stood there. He wouldn't go back even if he had the money. Why go pretend to mourn? Joe listened to a plane land, stared at the light coming in through the blinds. Slowly, he was overwhelmed with a feeling of uncontrollable sorrow. He sat down on the edge of his bed and sobbed quietly, not for his father's death, but for the fact that he was dead before dying. He cried not for his mother's loss of a husband, but for her loss of a life. He wept not for the loss of a father, but for the fact that he never really had one. Joe lay back on the bed, looked at the ceiling and thought about working with his Dad in the summer as a kid. He'd always wanted something from him, but it was never there. While they worked, Joe would try to talk, but it always ended up in an argument, sometimes with the back of a hand. There was some big hurt his Dad could never articulate, a hurt that ate away at him slowly until there was nothing left but bitterness. Anything but that life, Joe thought, anything at all. He got up, turned on the computer, found a poem he'd been working on, and finished it:

Having run out
of lies,
my father fights
the cool gray morning.
After Seagram's and O.J.
he loads the truck
with tools,
guns the engine,
and turns on radio news.
Today we will work
on old houses—
patch holes in walls,
mend fences
retile floors.

When the owners come
he'll talk shit,
jack the price.

Father, if I could
I'd take the sneer off
the face of the world,
bring back the lush green
fields of your childhood,
make the work simple and good.

Now there is only driving,
everyday harder,
a little less will.
We do not speak.
His hands covered
with tiny scars,
he steers the truck,
stares blankly
at the road.

Joe turned off the computer and went into the kitchen to make himself some coffee. He ground the beans, put the kettle on the stove, and leaned against the counter rubbing his swollen red eyes. He felt profoundly empty. The water was ready and he poured it over the grinds, taking in the thick, rich smell. When it was done, he stood in the kitchen and drank the coffee black. What do you do when your father dies? Joe looked at his hand on the mug—part of what made him was gone. He thought of his mother and wished her a new life. When things were over he'd try to talk her into moving out here. Joe finished his coffee and walked into the bathroom to take a shower. He stood under the water like a baptism. He would make something out of this; redeem his father through his own life.

After his shower, Joe dried off and put on his clothes. It was 11:00 A.M., Saturday. He remembered that he was supposed to meet Theresa outside Libros where she worked in Old Town. He walked into the bathroom and looked at himself in the mirror—tired with dark circles. Joe got his things together and headed out the door of his studio. It was quiet in the hallway and the sunlight glowed around the front door. He left the building and crossed Fifth Avenue to his car, got in, started it up, and turned the radio off. At Laurel, he turned left and cruised down the big hill without seeing the bay in the distance. He drove under the freeway overpass, turned right on Pacific Highway, rolled by the airport across Washington Street to the big parking lot at Old Town. As he pulled into the lot, he saw Theresa standing by the entrance to the Bazaar Del Mundo in a gauzy, white cotton *huipile* and a bright pink skirt. She smiled at him as he rolled down the window and waved. Joe pulled up next to her and she hopped in the passenger side. She was more beautiful than he had remembered. The scent of her lush black hair filled the car and her bright eyes shone like diamonds.

"How do you like my Conchita outfit?" she asked wryly.

"It's great," Joe said.

"I hate it," she said and laughed. "I'm gonna change at the beach. We're going to the beach, okay?"

"Sure, which one?"

"P.B."

Joe turned left on Taylor, crossed under the freeway bridge to Rosecrans, turned right on Sports Arena and felt the usual alienating, bland anxiety amidst the ocean of strip malls. He didn't say anything for several blocks until he stopped at a red light next to a massive SUV full of obnoxious children and Theresa put her hand on his arm and asked, "Are you alright?"

"My father died," he said flatly.

"When?" Theresa asked.

"Last night," Joe said as the light turned and he started up again.

"I'm sorry," she said, squeezing his arm a little.

"No, I'm sorry," said Joe. "Should I take you home?"

"Only if you want to," she said tenderly.

"No, I don't," he said as he stared at the road, "I need this."

Theresa gently touched the side of his face as he drove and, after some time, said, "You always had sad eyes. Sad, beautiful eyes."

She stroked his face and was quiet for quite some time as they hit Ingraham and made their way over the bay bridges. The water was glistening in the midday sun, and the horizon went on forever.

"Do you ever wonder what it would be like to go off in a boat, not knowing where you're headed," Theresa asked. "Just off into the blue sea to somewhere?"

"Anywhere," Joe said, "Anywhere new."

"Exactly," she said. Joe turned left onto Riviera, and drove by the shimmering bay, full of white sails.

"Can we stop by the park and walk to the ocean?" he asked.

"Whatever you want, Joe."

"Okay." Joe said as he drove to where Riviera dead ends into P. B. Drive, turned left on a side street, and stopped next to the small park by the bay.

"You know, I didn't love him," Joe said, staring ahead at the water.

"He wasn't good to you?" asked Theresa.

"He beat my mother. He wasn't *anything* to me though, not ever. Just a blank space in my life, a nothing. But he ruined my mother's life, killed the joy in her."

"That's hard," she said. "My ex-husband beat me for a year before I left him. Your mother probably felt like she deserved it somehow. It's hard to explain."

"What made you leave?" Joe asked as he turned to look into her soft brown eyes.

"My daughter. She needed a better life than that, somewhere

where she could feel whole," she said and looked down at her hands drawn together in her lap.

"How old is she?" Joe asked, putting his hand over hers.

"Five," Theresa said as she looked up.

"You're brave," Joe said looking still more deeply into her eyes. She smiled at him and squeezed his hand.

"I'm gonna go change," she said abruptly as she opened the car door.

"Okay," Joe replied. He watched her walk over to the bathroom, got out of the car himself, sat down on the hood, and gazed at the bay. People were rolling by in bathing suits and bikinis. Joe smiled a little as a very fat man in a Speedo rushed by on a skateboard with a tall-boy in his hand. Theresa came out of the bathroom in a pair of cut-offs and a plain black T-shirt. The sight of her made him feel light. She grabbed his hand, and they strolled down the walkway toward the Catamaran Hotel, past sterile white condos, quaint little cottages with pretty rose gardens, ugly brown vacation rentals, luxurious patios, and huge pools. They looked into people's windows as they went.

"I love to look into people's houses and imagine their lives," Theresa said. "It's a way to think about other lives I could have, other people I could be."

"And you take them all into yourself," Joe added.

"There are just so many lives, Joe, so many possible selves, you know?"

"And you want them all?" he asked.

"Yes!" Theresa laughed, "All of them, all at once!" Joe pointed out a man reading a book in an old leather chair. Theresa laughed at a woman in a pink leotard, sweating over an Ab Buster. They came upon the Catamaran and walked into the lobby past a family bickering in German and an elderly couple in matching yellow Ping golf hats, exited via the front entrance, crossed Mission Boulevard, and made their way through a bunch of teenage skate punks to the boardwalk. It was 1:30, and the beach was crowded. A woman on a mountain bike almost hit them as she whizzed by and rudely parted a couple in front of them. As always, Joe was struck by the ocean of tanned and toned flesh. He felt old, pale, and overdressed in jeans and a T-shirt. Still, there was a kind of wonderful, stupid, oversexed joy oozing out of the crowd. They came to a café, stopped for coffee, and found a good table next to a group of preening Italian women in skimpy beachwear and matching sunglasses.

"Que bella," Theresa said and smirked. They sat down, sipped coffee, and just watched people: a sunburned muscle man in a thong; a little red-haired girl on a new silver scooter; a crazy man in dirty flannel, dragging a bag full of garbage; a woman on a ten-speed in full racing gear; a Rasta man smoking a joint; a pair of tough kids with shaved heads and gang tattoos; a woman displaying her obscenely huge breast implants that poked out like rockets; a frail old woman in a Chargers jersey; a couple on roller skates kissing without stopping; people defiantly flaunting their imperfect bodies—too fat or too skinny, freckled and pale. Joe smiled and wondered if they ticketed such offenses. The Italian women got up to leave, and Joe watched their haughty saunter closely.

"Hey, teacher," Theresa interrupted, "Don't you get in trouble for that sort of thing?" Joe laughed and apologized.

"Don't worry, honey," Theresa said. "It's good for you. Here, I got you a present." She reached into her bag and pulled out a book of poetry, "It's Neruda."

"Thanks," Joe said. "You didn't have to."

"Let me read you a line," she said as she leaned over and rested her hand on his thigh. "Why is it so hard, the sweetness of the heart of the cherry?" Joe nodded slowly, took the book from her hand and read the rest of the poem.

"Is it because it must die or because it must carry on?" He closed the book and glanced at the back cover. It was Neruda's last book, *The Book of Questions,* written months before his death. Theresa kissed him on the cheek. Joe turned and touched the side of her face, gazed long into her eyes and thought, who is this other, this living mystery? When he kissed her lips softly, he closed his eyes, and the sounds of the boardwalk disappeared leaving only the lull of the ocean. Theresa pulled back gently, stood up, and took his hand.

"Follow me," she said. They walked away from the tables, back through the bustling throng on the boardwalk to the Surfer Motel. Theresa walked in and paid for a room without looking at Joe. The woman behind the desk smiled shyly at them. Theresa took the key and went over to the elevator, led them in, and stared up at the numbers as they ascended to the third floor. She walked out of the elevator without turning to him and made her way to their room to open the door. It was a classic sixties motor lodge—simple, funky, beach-themed. Theresa walked over toward the balcony, opened the drapes, unlocked the sliding glass door, and let the sound of the ocean pour in. Joe had seen it a thousand times, but now the vast sea blue sea unfolded before him like an unknown world, humbling in its majesty. When Theresa turned to him, she smiled and bent over to take off her shoes. Joe watched her undress slowly, peeling off her T-shirt, unclasping her bra, and letting her shorts and panties fall in a graceful dance. It filled him with desire but also reverence. Her naked body made the room sacred.

"Tell me, is the rose naked or is this her only dress?" she said as she approached him gently, kissed his forehead, and pulled off his shirt. Joe kissed her forcefully, passionately, lingering before stopping to explore the wonders of her body, kissing her neck, her shoulders, her breasts, her stomach, the insides of her thighs. She pushed him down, pulled off his shoes and pants, and mounted him, the forest of her thick black hair surrounding him as they kissed. When she pushed herself up, he slid his hands up her thighs to her beautiful wide hips, glanced up at her as she arched her back and moaned deeply. Her nipples hardened like miracles and he felt his spine tingle as they moved together, more quickly, then pausing, and resuming again.

After it was over, they lay together on the bed in the golden afternoon sun, just breathing deeply. Theresa leaned over, picked the book up off the floor and read, "Who wakes up the sun when it falls asleep on its burning bed?"

Joe smiled and said, "What did I do to deserve this?"

"Nothing," she said, "I chose you." He kissed her and took the book from her hand and read a line silently, "Was it where they lost me that I finally found myself?" He dropped the book on the floor and stared at Theresa lying beside him, smiling like an angel with her eyes closed. There is nowhere on this earth I would rather be, he thought. Nothing is more beautiful than the living, breathing heart of this moment.

18

Theresa cracked the door and looked in at her daughter as she slept peacefully in the moonlight. It was a warm night and she had one leg out from under the covers but was still clutching her old stuffed bear firmly in her arms. The day at her aunt's house had worn her out; there had been lots of other kids to play with. Her sister had had some fun with her when she stopped by to pick up Cecilia, nudging her when she saw a faint mark on her neck. "What kind of homework is this guy giving you?" she had asked her with a knowing smile. Theresa shut the door quietly and walked down the hall to the kitchen to grab a glass of wine. She found a glass on the counter in the shadows, poured a good portion of red, and stepped out on the back porch to get some air.

It was a clear night and the lights from downtown stood out crisply. This little house didn't have a lot of room or much of a yard for Ceci, but Theresa loved the view. Plus with the way rents were going up, where else could they move, even in Golden Hill? Theresa stared at the sign on top of the El Cortez, watched the name spell itself out, letter by letter in red neon, disappear and start again. She liked the deep rich red in the night sky, the endless repetition. Today she had gone outside of herself and the risk felt good. He had seemed more like a sweet, sad boy than her teacher, she thought. An ambulance blared by, speeding down Market toward somebody's pain. Theresa got a chill down her spine, took a sip of wine and looked up at the bank towers, empty except for the nightshift. Joe didn't seem to mind about Cecilia. That was encouraging. What was even better, though, was that she could say anything, be anything. The idea of making love in the strange room made her feel free somehow. It was like a space outside of time somehow, a new start. Theresa glanced at the freeway down the hill, the Coronado Bridge in the distance. She felt like the whole city was hers tonight. Every light was another person breathing, another heart beating, another soul hoping.

19 Alan was sitting under an elm tree at a table on the patio of a little coffee house in Old Town, tapping on his laptop, sipping cappuccino, and trying to wrap up the introduction to his book on tourism called *Learning from Living in a Mission Style Disneyland*. *"We are all tourists,"* he wrote, *"The old distinction between 'authentic' experience and 'commodified, inauthentic' experience is a false one. We all live inside the marketing, and claims of purity are the dying cries of an impossible way of being."* Alan watched a family walk out of a Mexican folk art store with colorful bags, stuffed with purchases. He took a sip of his double decaf cappuccino and continued to write: *"Even the purists who try to distinguish between authentic traveling and 'fallen' packaged 'tourism' cannot escape the fact that the forms of more authentic experience which they valorize are now marketed as well. One is sold the idea of 'adventure tourism,' and one's sense of intellectual, cultural, and existential/spiritual credibility is appealed to via the eco-tour, the 'outsider' guide, the cult of the 'in the know' countercultural traveler."* Alan stopped again, crossed his legs and observed a group of people leaving an over-the-top Mission style Mexican restaurant, giddy from margaritas. He smiled and wrote on: *"Once we leave the idea of an 'outside' of the tourist spectacle behind, we can distinguish four types of tourist. First, there is the 'First Class' type who frequents only the most expensive, exclusive, and carefully pedigreed spots. Her trips signify 'taste' in the classic bourgeois sense. Although in the hip 'new economy' a dollop of the avant-garde may accompany."* Alan took a sip of his double decaf cap, watched a sleek woman in black head into a chic mole restaurant. He continued: *"Next there is* the 'Rebel Tourist' whose entire experience is defined by pretensions of being beyond the guidebook and 'outside' of and in opposition to the marketing of experience. This bohemian type defines himself against the third type of tourist whom I shall call the 'Unapologetic Tourist.' This third type announces his boorishness gladly, refusing to experience anything that does not have an arrow pointed in its direction. 'Entertain me, I'm on holiday!' screams this recognizable fellow. Though frequently demeaned, one might actually consider this third type to be the most honest in his naïveté."* Alan stopped and frowned as a man in a Sea World shirt farted loudly at the table next to him. The girl from the coffee house asked him if he needed another double decaf cappuccino. He waved her away and started back up. *"Finally, we have the 'Postmodern Tourist' who has read the critiques, seen the victory of the commodity form to be complete, and continued on, not in opposition but with irony—gleefully consuming schlock and/or packaged authenticity with tongue firmly planted in cheek. This final type is a kind of wily interloper, moving freely between high and low, sacred and profane, with ease and humor."*

Alan stopped and closed his laptop. It was a beautiful day. Perhaps he would walk over to La Casa de Estudio to take some notes for the first chapter on Ramonaland in the new millennium. He wanted to finish his book fast and get it published. UCSD was a good place to start, but he'd love to get out of here, back to New York City where you didn't have to feel embarrassed for not wearing shorts and it wasn't shocking to find a good restaurant.

20   *When Herbert Marcuse came to San Diego in the late 1960s to teach at UCSD, he condemned the military industrial complex, the standardization of culture, and the corrupt, hypocritical nature of American life. He applauded the students for their "refusal to take part in the blessings of the 'affluent society'" and encouraged them to side with the disenfranchised, writing in* One Dimensional Man *that "It is only for the sake of those without hope that hope is given us." One student expressed his refusal like the Buddhist monks in Vietnam by burning himself alive in the middle of campus and leaving a note that said, "In the name of God, end the war."*

The Union-Tribune *bemoaned: "Marcuse calls for the Sabotage of U.S. Society," the American Legion offered the university $20,000 to buy out his contract, and someone hung him in effigy in front of*

City Hall with a sign that read "Marcuse the Marxist" pinned on his chest. The death threats rolled in from the Ku Klux Klan, the Minutemen, and other right-wing groups. "Like many of my colleagues who fought in World War II against the Nazis, I have begun to wonder whether Hitler was right," read one of the notes. "U.C. Professor flees home after Death Threat," cheered a Union-Tribune *headline. California governor Ronald Reagan and Vice President Spiro T. Agnew also joined in condemning Marcuse as an enemy of the state and corruptor of young minds.*

Marcuse, who decades earlier saw his friend and fellow Frankfurt School philosopher Walter Benjamin commit suicide rather than be captured by the Nazis, refused to back down. He occupied the Registrar's office with the students, continued to protest, and wrote of a revolution that would bring joy and full life in the place of injustice and suffocating conformity. On his long walks by the ocean, he dreamed that the people would choose ecstasy over rationalization. His office was full of figurines of hippos that he thought embodied absurdity and the possibility of the imagination. When he was forced to retire in 1969, Marcuse responded by saying, "What is at stake is the right and the duty of scholars and educators to teach the truth and expose lies."

21   Going to the publication party for *The Guerilla Phallus: An Anthology of Transgressive Endangered White Male Texts* was the last thing Joe was interested in, but Theresa was working late and he had promised his colleague Angie that he would go, so there he was, staring at an expensively framed photograph of an erect, elaborately tattooed penis sporting a painful looking piercing.

"Exquisite, isn't it?" said the host, a large, elegantly groomed man in J. Peterman catalogue wear with a booming voice. "It's our cover shot."

"It's great, Rex," Angie replied enthusiastically. "This is my friend, Joe. I teach with him at Central College." Joe extended his hand. Rex didn't take it, only managing to nod in a cursory fashion before heading over to another cluster of people he cared about more. Angie followed him across the room dutifully, chattering self-consciously. She was one of his former students and still under his sway. He had chaired her Master's thesis on Anaïs Nin's erotic writing and slept with her until his now ex-wife found out about it. Angie had seemed happy just to be graced by his attention, whatever form it took. She was a little naïve and overly impressed with Rex's "genius," as she called it. Rex had published several novels and edited the University of the Sun's literary journal. *Guerilla Phallus* was a special edition of the journal. His career had followed every trend from late sixties radical chic to postmodernism to nineties anti-PC reactionary to avant-porn. Joe picked up the advance copy of the journal lying on the entryway table and read from the introduction: "The Guerilla Phallus *is a collection of transgressive fictions and essays that contest the Politically Correct Establishment's demonization and marginalization of white male desire in the name of anti-sex feminist orthodoxy. It is our goal to liberate the oppressed white male phallus from the puritanical old girl's club that seeks to restrict everything from the 'male gaze' to the proliferation of affordable Viagra. Only when the phallus is free can the sensual imagination triumph and any form of truly liberatory politics flourish."*

Joe shut the anthology and strolled down the hall of Rex's house. The walls were decorated with pictures of Shiva, the Black Panthers, Frida Kahlo, and a heavily stylized sketch of a Japanese prostitute. He walked by an intense little man shouting, "The hegemony of jargon!" to a bored-looking woman in a black leather miniskirt who was smoking a joint with a studied ennui. She held the joint up for Joe as he passed. He took a hit, said, "thanks," and kept walking. He heard the woman say, "deterritorialized identities," as he reached the door to the patio. It was a warm evening, and there were various dyads and small groups chatting in the shadows. Joe stood by the door, looked up at the half-moon in the starless sky, and listened to the disembodied voices emerging from the darkness.

"I heard the old girls are after your Viagra," a woman's voice snickered. "What bullshit!" Joe took a few steps toward the garden and smelled roses blooming.

"I'm sorry, Alan, but you just don't know if you haven't been there," a man's voice insisted. "It's not about authenticity; it is authenticity! I've been to places you can't get to on a tour bus. When you're out there, all alone, with no help for miles, it's just you. That's not packaged, it's real. Just your soul and the mountain."

"Okay, Hemingway," another man's voice replied. "Whatever you say. You're just more real than the rest of us." Joe turned his attention toward the profile of a sleek young woman in the kitchen window. She was holding her chin between her thumb and her index finger as if for effect. Rex was leaning over her, looking calculatedly empathetic.

"Fuck California," Joe overheard in the distance. "New York City has more culture on one block than this whole pathetic theme park. Everybody's white, healthy, and Republican. It's like the body snatchers." Joe walked around to the kitchen door, peeked in, and saw that Rex and the woman had been replaced by a chubby, amiable-looking guy with thick black glasses and a fraying brown sweater. He was rummaging around in the refrigerator, looking for something.

"There's nothing but this Corona shit and wine," he said, smiling at Joe. "Intellectuals should drink thick, heavy beer with bold flavor. No wine in a box. That's an absolute no-no. My name's Martin," he said, stopping to shake Joe's hand. "Want a beer?"

"Sure," Joe said with an appreciative smile, "Whatever." Martin handed Joe a Corona Light.

"'Whatever.' It's a great word. It embodies our epoch. Are you one of the elitist ex-New Yorkers or are you a sycophantic graduate student?"

"Neither," said Joe and laughed. "I came with a friend."

"I'm the former. I teach at the University of the Sun, California Literature and Culture. You know, this place is full of case studies."

"Really?" Joe egged him on, amused for the moment.

"Well, there's Rex, the New York émigré who's embraced the flakiest aspects of sixties California counterculture while still maintaining a modicum of East Coast superiority."

"And?"

"The earnest Midwest transplants, the defensive natives. What particularly interests me, though, is the way it hasn't changed significantly from the days of Charles Fletcher Lummis and the first southern California bohemians. The leftism, the anti-leftism, the orientalism, the free love, the cult of the body, bohemians, middle class reds, beats, hippies, punks, new agers, suburban intellectuals . . . from the teens to the thirties to the sixties to now, it always gets repackaged. Look at this place—the peyote bowls, Kama Sutra figurines, Hopi art, Buddhas, the aria on the stereo, the health food snacks, the general patina of progressivism."

"And this means?"

"Fleeing from death in the sunshine."

"Unsuccessfully, I take it."

"Even with sex and God mixed in. And when it fails, it's disaster and apocalypse, then aimlessness, ennui. Life's no fun after the mystical orgy."

"I see," Joe said as he finished his Corona Light and set it down on the counter next to a plate full of half-eaten tofu wieners. He walked out of the kitchen and into the living room where Rex was holding court. Angie was sitting in a semi-circle with some of the graduate students, listening to him read a passage from Bataille's *Story of the Eye* out loud. It was like a perverse campfire group. Joe stepped out the front door for a moment and stood on the porch, staring down the empty suburban street with no sidewalks. All of the houses looked the same. He noticed that Rex drove a big red SUV and had a "Home Alert Security Systems" sign posted on his front lawn. Looking down, Joe spotted a note taped to a flowerpot under the porch light: "Manuel, please use the rakes instead of the blowers. The noise disturbs me. Tu Amigo, Dr. Rex." It was late and Joe thought about Theresa closing the bookstore and wished he were there to drive her home.

22 The weed and Corona Light from last night made Rex feel a little light-headed as he jogged briskly on the treadmill at the Mission Valley YMCA. It had been a good party; everyone was excited about *Guerilla Phallus*. He probably could have made it with Angie if she hadn't had to drive that boring guy home. Were they dating? What did she see in him? Rex panted as he put the level up a notch and stared in the mirror at the large breasts of the woman on the treadmill next to his. She caught him, and he looked up at the row of TVs above the mirror to avoid her recriminating glance. The Padres were losing on one screen and tech stocks were falling on another. Rex lowered his eyes, stared at himself in the mirror, and was overcome with a strange anxiety. The muffled sound of the aerobics class in the next room seeped through the wall, and he thought he heard the instructor say, "One, two, who are you?" Rex shook his head as he plodded on, uneasy over his mistaken hearing.

"Three, four, eternal door," he thought he heard.

"Five, six, River Styx," shrieked the woman's voice.

"Seven, eight, final fate," Rex thought he heard as he tried to laugh, but couldn't, still unable to shake the odd feeling.

"Nine, ten, unhappy end," he tried to block it out and looked in the mirror at the treadmill next to him, where the buxom woman had been replaced by a pallid anorexic girl in a black leotard. Rex could see the outline of her ribs poking through as the aerobics instructor shifted gears and began to bark out incomprehensible phrases.

"Angst in, angst in," said the voice. "Touch your darkness . . . death, death! Total darkness . . . death, death!" Rex felt a pain in his chest as he ran faster. In the mirror his face looked like a skull and the woman next to him was a sprinting skeleton. He turned the treadmill off quickly and leaned over it panting, almost unable to breathe as he fixed his gaze on the ground.

"Absurd, absurd . . . nothing inside! No, no! Nothing inside! No, no!" For a moment, Rex didn't know who he was. He felt an immense panic rising up inside of him and he wanted to scream.

"The sign says twenty minutes," said a woman's voice behind him. "Your time's up!"

23   Martin's head began to clear as he walked briskly around Chollas Lake, smiling at people as they passed by, watching the ducks floating peacefully on the sparkling water. He liked this little park. It was one of the few places in San Diego that had a vaguely Whitmanesque feel to it—diverse, working class, not just beautiful people. What a miserable party last night, he thought. Rex was such a blowhard and everybody worshipped him. The whole scene just made him want to get drunk and insult people. He did feel bad for that poor guy he had cornered in the kitchen. What had he laid on him? "Life's no fun after the orgy." What bullshit. Martin laughed softly to himself and nodded to an elderly Vietnamese man holding hands with what must have been his granddaughter, and winked at a little black kid trying to scare the ducks with a stick. A Mexican girl in a University of the Sun sweatshirt jogged by him and smiled. He could smell hot dogs cooking on a barbeque. Two Somalian women in beautiful green traditional dresses walked by cradling infants. This was the future of the city, he thought, of the state, of the country. It certainly wasn't Rex's crowd, not the beautiful people either.

Martin started another lap around the trail, and thought about his next project on the new immigrants and the reinvention of the California dream. Perhaps a good way to start it would be to invoke the Ramona mythology. Anglo boosters had come and constructed a mythological Spanish past while disenfranchising the Mexicans and Native Americans. Now the decaying Anglo paradise was being salvaged and reinvigorated by Latino, Somalian, Vietnamese, and other immigrants. Maybe a globalism angle would help, maybe a chapter on immigrant narratives, food, music, religion, place, and identity. Martin was almost run over by a little girl zooming by on her bike. He looked up at a man grilling *carne asada,* and playing games with his children. It smelled good and they looked happy. Perhaps at the end of the Anglo narrative of Eden turned to Apocalypse was a new story of rebirth. The Anglos had imagined a privatopia of "freedom from," a paradise of isolated individualism. These new immigrants believed in community; they brought it with them. But there was still the inescapable poverty, the racism, the inevitable competition for resources, the scapegoating. Hope or Apocalypse, maybe that's what he'd call it. Martin tried briefly to break into a slow jog, but his feet hurt and he just couldn't muster the energy. As he panted, the whole idea of starting a new book seemed futile. Who reads them? Why bother? He felt old and irrelevant. The whole world was moving beyond him. Forget it, he thought as he turned back toward his car, the freeway, his cell phone, the only common culture that bound him to others.

24 *The First Spiritualist Society of San Diego saw God in the sunlight. They built Villa Montezuma for concert artist and medium Jesse Shepard to play candlelight music and bring them closer to the one true source. Katherine Tingley dreamed of building "a white city in a golden land by the sundown sea" before building the School for the Revival of Lost Mysteries of Antiquity in Point Loma to house the Theosophists at the turn of the century. There, artists and others would practice yoga, paint, write, and connect with the World Soul. They borrowed wisdom from the classics of East and West, loved Shakespeare, the Vedas, and Swedenbourg. Up on the hill, above the gorgeous Pacific, there was hope for more than just material wealth. Even the young Henry Miller was drawn to the aura, fascinated by the Theosophist's retreat. San Diego with its eternal sunlight was the door to a new way of life where one realized the unity of nature and spirit and knew full life for the first time in the Golden West.*

in the music and on the street

25 Joe felt the weight of the dead semester fall from him as he drove down Park Boulevard past Frank the Train Man's, Casa Maya, and Buddhahead Furniture and Accessories before turning right onto El Cajon and rolling under the reddish-pink sign proclaiming "the Gateway to Midcity." He'd lost his one class at Central this summer and had no work, but that was all right. Time was enough. There was a little in the bank and the overdraft. He knew how to live cheaply and exist richly, he thought as he glanced over at a sushi restaurant in a strip mall next to a Mail Boxes Etc. and a 7-Eleven, crossed Florida Street, passed a Blockbuster Video, Mimi's Spa, a loan place, Livewire, Boulevard Liquor, and the Red Fox Room. It was early evening, but the sun was still bright and the air was warm. You have to own your own time, Joe thought, escape the prison of measured days and let moments emerge unhampered by expectations. He saw Dave's Flower Box, Dao Son Restaurant, a check cashing place, and a gas station at Texas Street.

The rush hour traffic was getting thicker, and Joe heard a car radio blasting a news story about a terrible accident involving a group of nudist firewalkers in East County. "They were all professionals, trained in the sacred arts," a voice said before disappearing into the distance. Joe caught the smell of grilled meat drifting out of Granger's Burgers and Ethiopian Café and continued on by the Berkshire Motel, Denny's, 31 Flavors, and the INS Application Support Center. He'd have to get something to eat before he met Mike and Theresa at the Pool Hall later. A city bus cut him off without signaling, and the little kids in the back window stuck out their tongues and laughed. Joe noticed that the teenage boys in the black Camaro in the next lane were staring at him, trying to look hard. He nodded to them but they only sneered back and peeled out without noticing the cop who then pulled them over. Two little boys were tugging on the side of their mother's dress as they waited at a bus stop. She swatted at their hands and reached into her purse for something. Joe met a woman's eyes in the rearview mirror of the Volkswagen in front of him and she glanced back briefly, probingly. There was a raw energy in the air as summer kicked and struggled to be born. Joe was hungry. He decided against Johnny's R Family Restaurant and pulled over in front of the Chicken Pie Shop at Oregon Street instead.

Inside the pie shop, Joe briefly stood next to a picture of a cartoon cow that said, "Eat more chicken," until he was seated by a weary looking woman whose Harley tattoo peeked out from under the back of her uniform, a pair of wings cresting just below her neck. She led him through the middle of the big open dining room past a table surrounded by an obscenely obese family and another occupied by a solitary old man in a wheelchair struggling to bring a spoonful of soup to his mouth. Once he was seated in a booth by the far wall, his waitress immediately came with a menu and said hello with a thick Russian accent and an unrehearsed smile. Joe already knew his order: chicken pie dinner, extra potatoes, chocolate pie, coffee. She took it and disappeared quickly into the kitchen. Joe watched the busboy clear a table in record speed, wipe it down, and move on to the next one. The old man was still laboring over his bowl of soup. Joe remembered how his grandfather never liked to eat out after his hands began to shake. This old man didn't seem to mind. He moved slowly, purposefully, stopping between spoonfuls to look about the room. There was a quiet dignity about the way he bore his loneliness.

The waitress came, flung Joe's dinner down abruptly, and quickly pushed her cart over to another table to deliver more pies. He watched the steam rise up off of the mashed potatoes, took a sip of black coffee, listened to clinking silverware, the cash register bell, and a the hum of a dozen conversations mixing as the dinner crowd grew. The food was filling and good. Joe ate it quickly, as if the pace of the place demanded it. He thought about the lives of all the people working and eating, the misery of the daily grind and the brief simple pleasure of chocolate pie. The couple in the booth behind him was bickering about money and the pair in front of him was chewing in silence, staring down at their plates.

A different waitress with a sad, hollow-cheeked and pockmarked face brought Joe the check while he was still eating his pie. She didn't look at him, turning instead to a busboy to say, "I never said table five, don't give me any shit tonight, okay?" Joe noticed that the old man had moved on to his dinner. He finished his pie, left a three-dollar tip for a six-dollar dinner, and made his way through the room to the register to pay the bill. A woman in a bus driver's uniform was playfully kissing her little girl on the cheek at the table by the front counter, and her whole face was glowing, transcendent with love. The people waiting in line looked tired, impatient, resigned. Joe paid his bill and walked out the door past another cartoon cow urging him to "Eat more chicken."

Outside it was twilight, Joe got back in his car and cruised by the Palomar Club, cocktails and card room, more strip malls, Wendy's, Burger King, Utah Street. He turned the radio on to the jazz station:

Dexter Gordon, "Body and Soul." He thought about his father's death, his own death still to come. Something led him back to the old man in the pie shop. Had he woken up one morning to find his beloved dead beside him, lost and alone after years spent together? Joe looked over at a thrift store closing up, Rudford's Diner, ABC Piano, a pawn shop, a yellow light at Thirtieth Street. He whizzed through it and noticed how the speed of his acceleration had coincided with the accelerated pace of the saxophone. The sky was getting redder, and he thought about the feel of Theresa's body against his, the smell of her hair, the taste of her sweat on her skin. There was a group of mourners going into Eternal Sunshine Mortuary, a drunk staggering out of Nightlife Nude Dancers, a woman posting the closed sign in Ida's Nails. Joe bopped his head to a heavy bass line in "Body and Soul" as a car pulled up beside him blaring rap and briefly drowning the jazz out before pulling away. What was the essence of Time? Joe wondered, as he drove past a somber crowd at a bus stop, crossed Illinois Street, and sped by a Hollywood Video, a Palm Reader and Tarot Card Psychic, a check-cashing place, Union 76, and another strip mall.

Joe hit Thirty-third Street and noticed that Dexter Gordon had turned into John Coltrane's "My Favorite Things." It was a live version that was faster, edgier than the studio one. Yet another check cashing place slid by, as did Venice Pizza, a used car dealer "Se Habla Español," an acupressure spot, and Capri Wigs. Joe was driving but felt outside of himself, somehow, in the music and on the street. Everything bled together seamlessly in the twilight and became part of the mystic fabric of impending night. He crossed Thirty-fifth Street and noticed a crowd of hipsters in front of the Zombie Lounge, smoking. They were a pastiche of historical references—forties swing, fifties rockabilly, fifties beat, sixties mod, eighties punk, twenties bohemian. A guy in a cowboy hat was leaning against an old mustang next to a woman who looked like Betty

Page. Both of them were talking to a guy with a goatee in a black turtleneck. The cowboy was wearing a Dead Kennedys T-shirt, blue jeans, and cowboy boots. Joe drove on past Anita's Flowers and North Park Produce and wondered if such depthless gestures had replaced the search for the new. He glanced over at Sam Lee Auto Repair, Chasers Cocktails, and a tattoo place and amused himself by imagining a series of tattoos that featured literary, cultural, and revolutionary figures: Whitman, Artaud, Ché. It had probably already happened.

Near Thirty-seventh Street, a prostitute was standing on the double yellow line in the middle of the street and nobody seemed to notice. Joe heard a shift in the tempo of the Coltrane piece, looked up at a "Year of the Dragon" banner hanging from a lamppost, watched a light go out in the Theosophy Building. There were some boys playing soccer in the dying light on the grass of the schoolyard next to an auto parts shop. Joe rolled by Dance World, Full Circle Yoga Institute, and the City Paint Store before crossing over the 15 Freeway. He saw a vacant lot through the eyes of a childhood memory, passed a police equipment warehouse, Imperial Oriental rugs, Vallarta Bar, and Pho Van Restaurant. There were Vietnamese and Thai signs everywhere. Joe thought to himself that there was a magic in unknown languages. The most banal message was filled with mystery. When you have no way into language, can you exist outside of it? Is there a more elemental way of knowing? Joe smiled as he saw the tipsy pink elephant on the T and M Liquor sign near Nguyan Hien Pharmacy, and Grace Community Church: Reverend Claude F. Eugene, Jr., Pastor. Joe listened to Coltrane's saxophone soar and was struck by the possibility of divine revelation coming to one in a storefront by a pharmacy and a liquor store. There was a kind of funky majesty to the idea that made him laugh out loud as he passed Auto Trek, Lloyd's Furniture, a pawnshop, a pager store, Thai House, the Ford Dealership, and Tweeter's Audio Video.

Coltrane left the structure of the melody and flew into some dissonant notes as Joe crossed Fairmont by the Labor Council, which made him think of Woody Guthrie. Etna Pizza, Asmara, Saigon Restaurant, Hoover High, and Kentucky Fried Chicken, "This land was made for you and me." There were some kids fighting on the street outside Near East Foods. Joe smelled a rich sweet odor wafting out of a Chinese Bakery, rolled on past Nam Bac Sam Nhugh Duoc, Chinese Herbs, Kon Luong, the Asian Business Center, Pho Hoa, 7-Eleven, and Euclid Street. "This land is your land," 97 Cent Discount Store, "This land is my land," Tony's Tire Shop, "This land was made for you and me." Coltrane made his way back into the melody and out of the tune as Joe passed Sam's Auto Body and a Jewelry Shop near Winona Avenue. Thelonius Monk's "Epistrophy" came on. Joe looked over at a small group of worshipers heading into Iglesia Pentacostales next to the TP Lounge and wondered at the sordid history of the Sea Breeze Motel. An ecstatic little boy was jumping up and down next to an ice cream truck pulled over on a side street. Monk's piano spoke to the last shred of light as it left the sky, filled the Minute Mart and the Chinese Food place with a blue feeling.

Joe drove on past Goodbody Mortuary, a 99 Cent Store, San Diego's Most Complete Sleep Center. Death, work, sleep, and dream, Joe thought as he kept going by a smog specialist, Morgan's Motel, Taco Bell, a car wash, Fifty-second Street, 7-Eleven, $3 haircuts, and Home Stretch rehab center where "Recovery is Possible," pulling over just past Fifty-third Street in front of College Billiards. It was 7:15. Mike and Theresa might already be here, he thought, coming out of himself, almost reluctantly, as he locked the door of his car and walked through the entrance of the pool hall and spotted them leaning on their pool sticks by a table in the far corner of the room. Theresa was listening intently to Mike as he spoke, gesturing animatedly, ignoring the balls on the table. Joe stood there for a moment and watched as Theresa nodded earnestly before walking over to a booth to grab her beer. Mike missed a tough bank shot and continued talking as Theresa calculated her next shot. She smiled at something he said, and her face lit up the room as she laughed. Joe smiled and headed over toward them weaving his way through the tables. A Vietnamese kid was practicing trick shots at one table, and two big guys in muscle shirts were grimly playing for money at another. As he came to the far table, Joe overheard Mike telling Theresa about an organizing drive he was working on at Inner Peace Market.

"The management has fired five workers, hired spies, and posted warnings at all three locations that say 'Someone's trying to divide the Inner Peace Family, but we won't let it happen.' It's like dealing with New Age Pinkertons."

"I see you two have met," Joe interrupted.

"Hey Joe," Mike said warmly, stopping to shake hands. Theresa walked over and kissed him briefly on the lips and put her hand on his arm.

"Mike is telling me union stories. It's like listening to my grandparents," she said teasingly.

"Your grandparents?" Mike asked.

"They were farm workers for almost their whole lives. I grew up hearing about strikes. They were both big union people. When I was a child I used to ask my grandmother why they hadn't just quit and gotten other jobs. She'd pat me on the head and say, 'because love and hope are hard work, *mija*.' I never knew what that meant until after they had died and I saw *Salt of the Earth*," she said self-effacingly and laughed. Mike nodded and looked impressed. He missed another bank shot.

"Were your parents union?" he asked.

"No, my parents ran a market before they retired, but they had the same spirit, always giving stuff away," Theresa said with a devilish look. Mike laughed and started in.

"But seriously, that's what matters, no? Love and community. What do we have without it?"

"Cars passing on the freeway," Joe chimed in.

"And suburbs of suburbs of suburbs full of houses with no sidewalks where people live in hostile isolation, calculating their debt and bitching about taxes."

"God bless America," said Joe.

"You know," Mike said with growing passion and seriousness, "in my worst moments I see clearly that it's a lost cause, but I keep working just because I want to keep the ghost alive. Haunt people with the idea that there's something larger than the market report, that it's not inevitable, that there could be something deeper and truer. Your family knew that."

"My grandmother would like you, Mike. Joe, does your friend always give speeches?" Theresa asked wryly. Mike smiled and missed a combination shot.

"I'm full of shit," he said.

"You certainly are, my friend," Joe said putting his hand on his shoulder tenderly. "I'm getting a beer."

"Get me her sister while you're at it," Mike said looking at Theresa wistfully and smiling. Joe walked across the room to the bar and glanced over at an intense looking guy with long stringy black hair in a plain white tank top and ripped jeans at the pay phone by the men's room. He had a tattoo of a skull and roses on his left shoulder blade.

"You said you were gonna bring the shit *here,* man" he hissed desperately into the telephone before looking around nervously. Joe looked away quickly and stepped up to the bar as the guy slammed the receiver down hard and ran through the maze of tables and out the door. Something about him inspired dread, Joe thought as he ordered a beer from the bartender, a sullen fat man with mean little eyes that addressed the world with a confirmed suspicion. Joe didn't need to say a word after his order. Just lay the bills down, the man's eyes said. As he made his way back to the table, he overheard Theresa say, "It means love is larger than yourself and freedom from it isn't freedom. It's a kind of denial."

"But some people define freedom as freedom from the burden of having a sense of a greater self," Mike responded, "And that's the problem." Theresa made a difficult bank shot, flubbed a much easier one and rolled her eyes toward the ceiling self-mockingly. Mike leaned over the table silently and measured a shot, decided against it, and stood back up to think. Joe noticed how the room suddenly seemed quiet, almost solemn.

"I think I'm gonna bail on the Casbah," Mike said, breaking the silence. "I don't feel ironic enough tonight."

"You sure?" Joe asked.

"Yeah."

"He's going home to be *very* serious," Theresa joked as she made the eight ball, stood up, and strolled over to touch his arm.

"It was great to meet you," Mike said, leaning over to hug her.

"Good to meet you, too."

"Take care," Joe said as they shook hands. "I'll call you next week." Mike nodded, put his stick against the wall, and headed toward the door. Joe watched him leave and began to rack the balls on the table.

"Is he okay?" he asked.

"Yeah. He's got a big heart. I like him," Theresa said.

"I know," Joe said as he watched Theresa break, sink a blue solid, and ponder her next shot. What surprised him about her, what he loved about her, was her uncalculated grace. She made a long shot and then sliced one into the side pocket. He hadn't known anything about her family before tonight. It struck him that it was just another part of what would be a long story. As he looked at her hand on the pool stick, the shape of her arm, the way her hair fell, he knew, at that moment, he had found something. When she missed her shot, he walked over, embraced her, and kissed her tenderly on the forehead.

"What was that for?" she asked.

"Nothing," he said. They finished their game and decided to leave. Joe paid for the table up front while Theresa was in the women's room. Outside it was dark. They got into the car and drove down El Cajon to Fifty-fourth Street, turned right and drove a few blocks to University and made another right. There was a blues show on the radio and Joe recognized an Albert Collins' guitar riff as they cruised by Almadina, a 99 Cent Store, and Roberto's #5 by Winona.

"I love that place," Theresa said as they drove by the Egyptian style Big City Liquor and crossed Euclid into City Heights and a rush of Asian markets, the Kitty Kat Adult Theatre, and a karate studio.

"Me too, it's unexpected there, a jewel amidst storefronts. Too bad they had to chop the tower off of the Tower Bar next door," Joe replied.

"Yeah, I remember that place. I guess they only save landmarks in the Gaslamp," Theresa said as they cruised by La Especiale Produce, Save U Foods, and Quoc Te Vietnamese Restaurant.

"Hey, look, it's Li, from class," Theresa said as they rolled to a stop at Fairmont.

"I didn't see him," Joe said as he scanned the blackness behind him in his rearview mirror.

"He was taking out the trash in front of that restaurant back there. I talked to him a couple times before class. Did you know he was a refugee?"

"No," Joe replied as they continued on past George's Coffee Shop, Oscar's Cocktail Bar, Forty-second Street, and the bridge over the 15 Freeway. R.L. Burnside was on the radio, grinding it out.

"It must be fascinating sometimes, seeing all of the people you see when you teach, guessing at their stories," Theresa said after a long silence.

"It is," Joe replied. "There's always much more that you don't know than you do. You only ever get past the tip of the iceberg with most people, then it's over and you start all over again with a new set of questions." He put one hand on her leg as they rolled past more storefronts, Oriental Garden Massage, Canada Steak, the Star and Garter strip club, San Diego's Finest 24-Hour Donuts, El Uno Bar, and Happy Daze Liquor at Wabash Avenue.

"Well I'm not a question anymore," Theresa said. "Now you're driving through the night with me. Who would have imagined?" Joe smiled but didn't say anything as they drove by the San Diego Rescue Mission Thrift Store, the Thrift Store Alliance for the African Alliance, the 88-Cent Price Breakers, King's Office Supply, Thirtieth Street, and the North Park sign.

"Have I told you that driving makes me horny?" Theresa said playfully as they passed Big City Tattoo.

"No," Joe said, glancing over at her as they went by Tobacco Rhoda's.

"Yes, but don't get too excited yet. I like to milk the feeling." They laughed and drove by the F Street Bookstore, under the bridge before Park Avenue, and entered Hillcrest. Koko Taylor's "I'd Rather Go Blind" came on the radio as they made their way past storefronts flying rainbow flags, a deluxe Mission-style strip mall, Condoms Plus, Tokyo Blonde, Euphoria, Whole Foods, two Starbucks, and the neon Hillcrest sign by Jimmy Wong's Golden Dragon. Joe listened to Taylor's voice stretch just up to the point of breaking and nodded along as the guitar wept in unison, so bittersweet it tugged at something deep and almost painful. Theresa glanced over at two men dancing in cowboy outfits on the sidewalk outside of Kickers. At Goldfinch, Joe turned left and sped down the long dark street to

125

Laurel, turned right, and rolled under the 5 Freeway before making another quick right at Maple to park in front of a row of tiny World War II era bungalows behind the Casbah.

"So, what are we seeing?" Joe asked as they walked around the corner alongside the apartments above the club where whole families struggled to sleep through freeway noise and rock shows, seven days a week.

"El Vez is the closer," Theresa said. "I don't know who the first two bands are." They pulled out their IDs at the front door, and Joe picked up the cover. The place was packed and he was struck by the mishmash of styles as he and Theresa weaved their way through the crowd smoking on the patio just inside the front entrance—lounge, hip hop, grunge, punk, rockabilly, surfer, swing, disco, glam, etc. Joe noticed a Mexican guy with a garish eyebrow piercing in a red beret and a white undershirt. He had a tattoo of Che Guevara on his bicep. Inside, the first act was finishing up. It was a black guy who seemed vaguely autistic banging on a keyboard, singing a one-line song to a great amount of mock enthusiasm. Joe wasn't sure the performer got the joke.

When the song ended, the crowd whooped loudly and Joe overheard someone say, "You know he was actually homeless when they found him. He's got three CDs now." Theresa shot Joe a knowing look, and they waded over to the bar to order drinks. Two vodka sodas. Theresa took a sip of her drink and put her arm around Joe's waist. They made their way to the far wall, leaned back, and watched people. A guy in a bowling shirt was making a move on a woman with a shaved head in a polka dot miniskirt. Next to them, a group of pale, languid twenty-somethings in black leather were silently sipping mixed drinks. Joe overheard someone say, "Who gives a shit if I voted for a Republican? Politics bore me." When he turned around he saw a guy dressed like a character from *The Beverly Hillbillies* casting a pleading look at a Courtney Love look-alike.

The next act came on. They were a cowpunk band that did sped-up versions of TV theme songs. Joe tapped his foot to a rockabilly version of *The Jetsons,* and laughed out loud at a hardcore rendition of *The Waltons.* Theresa tried to guess what a couple of songs would be in advance, but lost interest after a number or two. As they went into a Hank Williams-style *MASH* theme song, Joe wondered if it took more cleverness or banality to create an art form utterly devoid of affect. Amazingly, the band's repertoire included over twenty covers. Joe tuned out and watched a guy in Hawaiian beachwear and camouflage Converse sneakers order a beer and look longingly at Theresa. In the mirror behind the bar, the faces were bored, mildly amused, cynical, knowing, all-too-knowing. When the music stopped, it was a relief to hear the Replacements come on the jukebox behind the din of conversation. Theresa went over and bought them two more drinks. She was wearing jeans and a plain black T-shirt, and the simplicity stood out in stark contrast to the self-consciousness all around her. Joe looked down at his own green shirt and old jeans and no tattoos and felt old.

Theresa came back with the drinks just as El Vez came on. He opened with a Spanish version of "Mystery Train" that broke into an improvised "Mexican Revolutionary Train" riff. The El Vettes behind him were in lurid red dresses. At least it was multicultural irony, Joe thought. Theresa looked over at him probingly, and he said, "They're funny, really." El Vez broke into a seventies Elvis version of "Jailhouse Rock," purposely limiting the range of his voice and stripping off his jacket to reveal a T-shirt with a picture of The King shaking hands with Richard Nixon. "Gracius, Gracius," he slurred after the sloppy rendition was over. As they began a campy version of "Love Me Tender," Joe glanced over at the poster listing the upcoming events: punk rock karaoke, Hank Williams III, Rocket from the Crypt. "Love Me Tender" morphed into "Viva Las Vegas" and Theresa touched his arm and said, "Let's go."

Back in Joe's apartment they made love in the dark, exploring each other's bodies as if they were blind. Theresa stood still as Joe trailed his tongue down through the middle of her shoulder blades to her buttocks and then around curve of her hip to the nub of her pleasure and stayed there until her legs melted and they fell to the floor.

As he entered her, she noticed how they moved together with ease now, nothing awkward. Then the feeling built, and she stopped thinking, nursing the exquisite line between aching and ecstasy for what seemed like a long time until it broke and everything was fluid and full, as if her being was ripe to blossom. When she came, it was so hard that she wept and dug her fingers into his back. He kissed her then and licked the tears from her cheek as he finished slowly but intensely, and she came again, but more softly like an aftershock punctuating the moment.

"I love you," Joe told her as a late plane flew over, drowning him out.

"What?" Theresa said.

"I love you," he said again.

"I heard you that time," she answered stroking his hair softly. "Me too."

After Joe was asleep in the bed, Theresa lay next to him and listened to his breathing. She wondered if Cecilia had had a good time at her aunt's house. How would Joe do with her? He was a kind man, but not everybody understands children. She couldn't keep shipping her to her aunt's house forever. Another late plane flew over and Joe tossed a bit in his sleep. She stroked his back a little and he settled down. For a moment, she tried to imagine them all living together in the same house, like a family, but she stopped herself. Don't go writing any fairy tales, honey, she thought. Right now it's just good to have sore muscles in places you'd forgotten about. Just let it unfold, she told herself as sleep began to spill over her, just let it happen.

Theresa dreamed of driving with Joe through a vast, empty space. Cecilia was in the back seat smiling sweetly as Joe made funny faces for her. They were surrounded by brilliant light everywhere, glowing white-hot light. It was no place she'd ever seen, and the car kept moving faster. Joe and Cecilia didn't notice the speed, and they couldn't hear her warnings. Even when she grabbed Joe's arm violently, he didn't feel it. After a while, he turned his head to her and said, "I love you." The car was surging forward, plunging into a blank nothing. Suddenly, they hurled into a wall, and the car was crushed to half its size. Miraculously, Theresa was not hurt, but she was covered in blood. Joe's head had plunged through the windshield and Cecilia had smashed the side of her face into the passenger side window. Theresa couldn't unlock her seatbelt. She screamed but there was no one to hear her, no one but the two of them, bloodied and lifeless in the menacing light. When she woke up, Theresa was gasping for air. Joe was still sleeping peacefully beside her, so she put her arm around him and pulled herself tightly to his side, listening to his breathing, groping for the beating of his heart.

a jewel amidst storefronts

26

Mike watched a couple stroll toward the back door of the Dolphin Inn. He was the only one left in the place. Big Dog waved to the couple as they left, nodded to Mike and began to tune his guitar. The rest of the band left the stage and walked over to the bar to get drinks. Mike knew what was coming next. When the place was dead, Big Dog would play long slow numbers to the empty room. Something about it struck Mike as beautifully pure. As Big Dog tentatively strummed some plaintive cords, Mike contemplated his own loneliness, feeling its raw edge as he explored the contours of his despair. It was beyond politics, beyond the personal. He felt like the world had emptied out somehow, emptied him out. He veered between the void and anger until he reached a strange, precious trembling and felt alive. Just as the solitary notes of the guitar occupied the silence bravely, there were moments of full life. Mike took a sip of his beer, watched intently as Big Dog closed his eyes, dug in, and made the guitar weep. He cradled the instrument so closely to his massive frame that it almost seemed to disappear into his body, become a part of it. But it was his face under the old black fedora that held the stories. There must be a hell of a tale, Mike thought, for every deep line and gray hair.

Big Dog opened his eyes for a moment and noticed the white guy at the bar was still there. He had a heavy sadness to him that made you feel like speaking in a whisper. The music seemed to be working on him though, pulling him through it. Big Dog closed his eyes again and improvised a blues solo based on "On the Waterfront." He didn't feel like singing, so he let the guitar talk. He thought about going fishing tomorrow off the pier in Imperial Beach, maybe going over to Deanna's afterward. The doctor told him he should stop staying up late, but fuck that. He'd play until he died on stage. He'd spent forty years in barrooms from Mississippi to California and never been able to save a dime. What else was there? He could make people happy, help them work their shit out at the end of the day. What was the use of sitting in his house at night watching TV? Big Dog stretched it out a bit longer and surprised himself a little with a riff that just came to him out of nowhere. Sometimes you just hit the spot, he thought, do the same old shit in a new way for the thousandth time. "What the hell you doing!" he heard the drummer yell and laugh. When he finished, the white dude got up to leave and waved good night. Big Dog waved back and said, "Thank you." The rest of the guys were already packing up. He put his guitar in his case, said goodbye to them and Norma behind the bar, and walked out to his car. Driving down Market, he felt bone tired, lonely, and hungry for some late-night breakfast. He kept his eye on some pipe heads running across the street in front of him while he waited at a red light. As he got closer to downtown, the skyline appeared in the distance and it felt like anything could happen even though everything was closed.

27 Li finished cleaning the stove and walked over to the sink to wash up. His father had gone home for the evening and left it to him to close the restaurant. He struggled against his irritation, remembering all the years his father had done the same. Just sweep, just clean, just wash, he told himself. When he was finished, he shut off the light in the kitchen, grabbed his coat, set the alarm, locked the back door, and stepped into a dark alley.

Out back, Li heard bottles clinking and saw a pair of legs sticking up out of a dumpster, the feet moving back and forth as if struggling to walk on the air. He double-checked the lock and strolled down the alley, trying to clear his head. He thought about the rude woman who insulted him, sent back the food, and refused to tip. He thought about the man who leered at his sister as he ate. "A nice little fuck," he had said to his friend. And then, "Don't worry, they barely speak English." He thought about having to come back tomorrow, and it filled him with dread and anger. When he came to the end of the alley, he passed by a man sitting on the sidewalk against the wall, drinking from a bottle of liquor in a paper bag. The man smelled wretched and even in the dim streetlight Li could see the filth on his jacket.

Li turned right down a lightless side street. He walked slowly, feeling his feet on the ground, giving himself up to the movement of his legs until he was centered. In his mind's eye, he could see the emerald-blue lake he had discovered with his father on their hike last summer in the high Sierras. Father had been telling him about the Way, not about books or sermons dealing with it, but how, as a young man, he had come to it without them. They were in step with each other, breathing hard, and the rhythm of their hearts was steady. It was then, just as they ascended past the tree line, that the lake had revealed itself to them, bathed in ethereal sunlight, like all of eternity in one second. Li stopped walking, savored the memory as it faded, and noticed that the street was quiet. He concentrated on his breathing for a moment, tilted his head back, and opened his eyes to see the jewel of the moon, circled by clouds in the June night sky.

28

Gary pushed open the front door to College Billiards and stepped out onto El Cajon to flag a cab. He could feel the last bit of his high fading fast, and it was making him desperate. Tommy was supposed to have met him with the stuff but he didn't show. Now he had to meet Edgar at work and get a ride to the beach to pick it up. What bullshit. Gary waved his hand frantically at an approaching cab. Pilgrim Cab, never heard of them, whatever. It pulled over quickly and he hopped in back.

"Eternal Sunshine Mortuary," he said.

"Mortuary?" the cab driver asked with a heavy accent that sounded African.

"Yeah, just turn around and I'll tell you when to stop," Gary snapped. The cab whirled around, and the driver made a reckless U-turn, resulting in several prolonged honks.

"Careful buddy," Gary snapped again, his heart pounding. He looked at the driver's ID posted on the dashboard—Ahmed something. Just my luck, Gary thought, a black Muslim. He's probably a terrorist hiding out until his suicide bombing. The guy drove down El Cajon like a maniac, weaving in and out of traffic. Gary held on to the door handle and ground his teeth.

"God damn it," he said to himself.

"What did you say?" the cab driver asked sharply, glaring at him in the rearview mirror.

"Nothing man," Gary replied hostilely, "Just drive, okay?"

"What do you know about God?" the cab driver shot back.

"Nothing, I don't know A-N-Y-T-H-I-N-G" Gary snarled, "Can't you just drive, man!"

"I can drive," he said looking back again, more probingly than angrily this time. "Are you all right, my friend?" he asked as he came to a sudden stop at a red light.

"What?" Gary asked incredulously, "Are you fucking crazy or something? Don't fuck with me, all right? Just stop the car and let me out here. It's only one more block. I can walk."

"We are stopped," the cab driver said.

"Whatever. How much?" Gary barked.

"Five dollars." Gary gave him five with no tip, jumped out of the car, dashed across the street and hurried down the block to the mortuary where he rushed inside to find Edgar on the phone in the little office by the lobby, consoling a client about his loss with his official voice.

"We'll do everything we can to ease the process, sir. Try to get some sleep." Edgar hung up, and Gary sat down in a plastic chair bathed in the eerie fluorescent light that made the office seem like heaven in a TV skit. There was nobody else there. Edgar worked the night shift when the elderly couple that ran the place was gone or asleep upstairs in the living quarters. Gary was particularly happy not to see Lonnie the embalmer there. He'd do a couple lines with them and start going off about the film *Harold and Maude*. He'd seen it hundreds of times and was always asking them to come over to his house and watch it with him. Once Edgar had had to go downstairs to ask Lonnie a question, and he caught him burning incense, standing nude next to a cadaver, also nude. Edgar never asked the question, and Lonnie had just smiled at him and said, "We're all just meat in the end."

"Hey what's up, Gary?" Edgar said in his normal voice.

"When can we get out of here?" Gary asked urgently.

"I have to make a few more calls, and then I can set up the answering machine for the rest of the night. The old geezers are away for the weekend."

"How long?" Gary insisted.

"Not long. Here, chill out," Edgar said as he opened the desk drawer and pulled out a mirror with four lines on it. "Knock yourself out, but leave two for me. That's all I have left." Gary picked up the half-straw, leaned over and did one line fast, sat up briefly with his eyes closed, bent back over and did the other line. They evened him out, took the edge off.

"This message is for Mrs. Frankel. My name is Edgar Ramirez, calling from Eternal Sunshine Mortuary. While we know that the death of a loved one is trying for everyone, your last payment is past due—" Gary got up and walked into the entryway, out of earshot. He looked at the plastic flowers by the door and glanced over into the little chapel reserved for on-site services. He wondered if the clients knew that this place was a money mill. Once he had come to meet Edgar here after his shift was over and overheard the old couple joking that they were atheists but that God was good for business. Gary didn't know about God. He felt the burning in his nose subsiding, and the strange, almost metallic taste of the meth reached his tongue.

"Let's go," Edgar said cheerfully as he emerged from the office. "The bereaved can leave a message." They walked out onto the street to Edgar's car, and something about a passing bus filled Gary with anxiety. The two lines had stopped the bleeding, but he needed more. He sat in the passenger's seat quietly, feeling disengaged as they drove to the freeway, the streetlights and cars passing in a blur. The freeway was better somehow, more open, freer. He liked the red of taillights. Edgar was quiet too, driving intently, snorting occasionally until he said, "I hope it's not another ugly scene over there. Tommy's got some fucked-up friends."

"Yeah, I know. But what can I do if he'll never drop it off?"

"Drug addicts—you just can't rely on them," Edgar said wryly. "They never think of anybody but themselves." Gary didn't answer. He just stared out the window at the deep dark water as they cruised over the bay bridges, turned left after the second one, and drove down Riviera until they came to Tommy's dumpy Fifties-style apartment complex, surrounded by newer, vastly more expensive condos. It was like someone had forgotten to tear it down. Edgar parked across the street, and they followed the sound of Metallica blasting until they found Tommy's apartment, ignoring the suspicious stares of a few neighbors on the way in. The door was open and the big couch was crowded with people Gary didn't recognize—a tough Mexican guy with a shaved head who looked like a gang-banger and had the tattoos to prove it, an overly tan blond guy in fancy clothes wearing what looked like a Rolex, a surfer dude in a bathing suit and flip-flops, and some other dude in a 7-Eleven shirt and a Padres cap. Nobody was talking except the surfer. He was in the middle of a long discourse about waves. The guy with the tattoos was grinding his teeth hard and nodding. The other two looked distracted.

"Where's Tommy?" Gary interrupted.

"In the other room," said the Rolex guy. Gary and Edgar walked by the bathroom door past what sounded like the muffled shouts of an argument and found Tommy sitting on the edge of his bed smoking some shit out of a glass pipe. He was naked, and there was a dark haired woman lying next to him with her bare legs flopped open, exposing her vagina. She looked at Gary and Edgar and smiled a lurid smile full of malice. She laughed at Gary's surprised expression. He thought it was strange that she still had her top on. It was hard to see her clearly in the dim, shadowy light, but he got the impression that she was middle-aged.

"Sorry about the mix-up," Tommy said as he exhaled. "Want a hit?" Gary grabbed the pipe and the lighter and took a long one. He could feel the rush swelling as he sucked in the smoke.

"It's ice," Tommy said. "It'll blow your head off." Gary passed the pipe to Edgar who looked a little reluctant but did it anyway.

138

His eyes got big as he exhaled and he had to sit down on the floor. Gary handed Tommy a wad of bills just as the phone rang. The machine picked it up. It was the manager complaining about the noise. Tommy walked into the other room without covering himself and turned the stereo off. He told the guys on the couch they had to go and opened the bathroom door to shoo out two more "friends" who looked like they were on the verge of a fistfight. Once they were all gone, he locked the front door and pulled back the heavy bed sheet that covered the front window to survey the courtyard—nobody there. Back in his room, he turned on the police scanner but there was nothing but a DUI and a bar fight. Tommy turned the scanner down and motioned to Gary and Edgar to follow him into the other room. They all went into the living room, and Gary noticed that his body was still tan and well muscled from his football days at Texas Tech. You'd never think he'd been high for who knows how long if it wasn't for the black circles under his steel blue eyes. Other than that, Tommy had a kind of innocent look about him, almost naïve. Gary had always thought it was funny that his dealer looked like the all-American blond boy. Maybe that's why he never got busted. "You guys want to fuck her?" he asked matter-of-factly. "I picked her up off the street a couple days ago, and she's been fucking for hits all night."

"I don't know," said Edgar.

"Let's just get high," Gary agreed.

"Okay, I'll just be a minute. Take the pipe," Tommy said amiably. Gary and Edgar sat down on the couch and did a few more hits. The shit hit them like electric jolts and lit them up. They talked furiously about nothing for what seemed like a long time. Then Edgar started talking about going back to school and finally making something of himself. He was going to be rich, fucking big. He'd make his mother proud. Gary noticed the sound of flesh slapping in the other room. There was no moaning though. He got up to pee and saw

Tommy's backside rising and falling frantically when he glanced into the dingy bedroom. For some reason, he thought it was weird that there was nothing on the walls and almost no furniture. In the bathroom, he peed and looked at himself in the mirror. His image startled him. Was that his ashen gray face? Were those his red eyes surrounded by black circles? Was that his dirty, stringy black hair? He didn't care. He stopped looking at himself and headed back toward the living room.

"Hey you!" said the woman in the in the bedroom, almost tauntingly. "Come in here so I can suck your dick." Gary walked into the room without thinking about it and stood by the bed. The woman had taken off her top and her large sagging breasts were sporting long, hard nipples.

"Let's see if you can do better than your friend," she said sarcastically as she unzipped his pants and started to give him head. He got hard quickly, but his excitement was distant somehow, like he was someone else. He noticed that the woman was biting him roughly but he didn't mind it. Soon he was on top of her, working away quickly. He felt like a machine that could go forever. The woman's body was trembling beneath him, but he couldn't tell if it was from the speed or pleasure. Gary noticed that Tommy was sitting on the ground against the wall in the corner of the room watching him, weeping. He tried to ignore him and, after a while, Tommy got up and left.

"Make me come, you bastard," the woman hissed at him. "Harder!" Gary did it as hard and fast as he could and slowly, after what seemed like forever, he felt the pleasure rise in his groin. The woman beneath him opened her eyes widely and gritted her teeth.

"Not yet," she said. Gary held out for a while until he felt her move her back spasmodically and her whole body shook in a way that made him think she might be having a seizure.

"Get off me," she said as he came, "Get the fuck off me!" Gary got up and walked into the bathroom to rinse himself off in the sink. There was bright sunlight streaming in through the little window in the shower. When he was done, he went out into the living room to find Tommy sobbing on the couch. Edgar had bailed on him.

"Help me," Tommy choked through his tears. "You're my friend, right?" Gary could hear the woman on the bed laughing out loud. "Send the baby back in for some lovin'," she yelled mockingly, "Mama'll make it all right." Something about her laughter chilled Gary to the core, made him hate her, hate himself. Tommy buried his head in his hands and whimpered, "Get the fuck out of here, please." Gary obliged, picking his baggie of meth up off of the coffee table by the couch and stepping out the front door into the blinding glare of the sun. He was still high as a kite. One of the neighbors stared at him suspiciously through a window, so he walked out of the courtyard quickly and decided to head down to the beach by Mission Bay. There were pretty young girls jogging on the sidewalk and an old man was walking his dachshund. Gary made his way to the beach and sat down on the warm sand. It felt unreal. A couple walked by with their three small children. One of them squealed loudly and it made Gary wince. He noticed that his heart was still racing wildly. It was a high without feeling, this one. He felt like a corpse washed up on the beach.

29 Ahmed watched the crank head run across the street toward the mortuary. How sad, he thought, running headlong toward death without God, without hope. The light turned green and he drove on toward Park Boulevard, not thinking about where to go. *Empty the glass of your desire so that you won't be disgraced,* he thought, remembering a poem by Rumi. Ahmed glanced over at a man pushing a shopping cart by a Mercedes Benz at a stoplight. *The Man of God is a King clothed in rags,* he said to himself. Then he got a call to pick up a man in University Heights and take him to the airport. He raced toward Park, turned right, and weaved his way through traffic and tried to remember how to get to the street. *The Man of God sees good and bad alike,* he thought, as he turned around after guessing the wrong street. Ahmed ignored another call from the dispatcher telling him to hurry up and get there. It was a nice warm night and he was happy. *The man of God has a hundred moons at night,* he remembered as he finally found the right street and began to search for the proper house. When he saw a man in a business suit standing in a driveway he came to a screeching halt.

"It's about time," the man said curtly, "If I don't make this flight, your boss is going to hear about it." Ahmed didn't respond to the man's tone, saying only, "Good evening, sir, which airline?"

"United, now step on it!" the man ordered him brusquely. Ahmed sped toward Washington Street and down the hill toward the airport. *When the earth is this wide, why are you asleep in a prison?* he thought as he glanced in the rearview mirror at the man who was bickering with his wife on a cell phone. Ahmed turned left onto Pacific Highway and watched the man grimace as he turned off the phone.

"Are you all right, sir?" he asked.

"Just drive the car and mind your own business," the man snapped. Ahmed said nothing more. He whizzed down Laurel to Harbor Drive and the airport, getting the man to his gate in time.

"Next time make it easier on yourself and get there on time," the man said as he paid his fair and thrust an extra dollar at him. Ahmed watched him walk away into a crowd of other rich, hurried, miserable people. For a moment his mind traveled back to Mogadishu and all the suffering he had seen there. It made him smile at the absurdity of these Americans with so much of everything and so little wisdom or charity. He drove around the loop out of the airport and back onto Harbor. The water was beautiful in the moonlight this evening, and the warm air caressed his skin like velvet. *The man of God is far beyond non-being,* he said to himself, *The Man of God is seen riding high.*

30   *It was a mistake, the product of a vulgar utopia gone awry. At the turn of the century, they dreamed of transforming the desert into a garden by bleeding nature of more than she readily offered. When they sought to divert the waters of the Colorado, they flooded downhill and formed the Salton Sea. In the wake of this disaster, they dreamed of turning the floodwaters into their own depraved version of Eden, a haven for real estate boosters, businessmen, and all the hungry failures who had lost out on the golden dream in Los Angeles and San Diego. But everything went wrong, and all the detritus of the dying dream flooded into the sea—all the pesticides, toxins, organic compounds, and salt, salt, salt mixed together to form an ocean of poison that is killing even the hardy corvina, who survived, like those who transplanted them, by eating all the smaller fish. Now the fish lie rotting by the shore, easy prey for the birds that scoop them up hungrily and die in huge numbers.*

It started in 1992 with thousands of dying grebes, then came the ducks, followed by the white and brown pelicans. A die-off in the late nineties vanquished over 20,000 birds, and it just keeps happening. All of this in one of the last great migratory stops for birds in the Western United States, where the officials can do little more than collect the birds to burn them in huge incinerators, making the refuge a kind of absurd avian concentration camp where animals come for easy food and end up dying from the gruesome diseases that lurk in the sea's dark waters.

everything from the dirt to the stars

31

Theresa was dreaming of swimming freely in an endless sea of water so deep blue that she couldn't see her arms moving in front of her. She was lost, utterly unmoored, but unafraid as she moved gracefully about with no purpose. Slowly, a light appeared, and she was drawn toward it. As she ascended, the water lightened to a wonderful azure, and she noticed that, strangely, she could breathe. Further up, it became translucent, and the sun gleamed above her. She had a sense that her naked form was part of the ocean, almost inseparable from it. Then, slowly, she began to dissolve into it quickly, too rapidly for her to reach the surface in time. There was a boat above her and she could see faces looming, looking down, searching the depths for her. At first the voices were loud and persistent, calling her name, then they faded, and she dispersed happily, into the welcoming fluid forever. When she woke up, she was smiling oddly in the passenger seat of Joe's car, unaware of the swarm of traffic surrounding them, zooming east on Interstate 8 toward the desert. She heard a voice on the radio speaking Spanish, followed by a translator, "The mask is a mirror. If you look closely enough, you will see yourself. I am you." While her eyes were still closed, the newscast switched from the story about the Zapatistas to a piece about the little known costs of globalization. The reporter was interviewing a United Nations commissioner named Kevin Bales who informed him that, by his estimate, there were twenty-seven million slaves in the world today, but that others put the number as high as two-hundred million, more than in the nineteenth century. Theresa opened her eyes and looked over at Joe, who was patiently waiting as an SUV jammed in front of him without signaling.

"What did you dream?" he asked her with a smile.

"That I dissolved into the ocean," she replied sleepily.

"Without me?" he responded. Theresa put her hand on his arm and listened to another story about Operation Gatekeeper and yet another about a local man who had disappeared into the desert without a trace.

"It's like a nightmare machine," she said, pointing to the radio. Joe switched to a rock station that was advertising cell phones and then to another station with a commercial for on-line trading. Theresa leaned over and turned the radio off.

"I'm serious," she said. "It's like we have machines to do our dreaming for us. Our inside is outside, you know? And we just get pumped full of garbage and our dreams die."

"Okay," Joe replied, "We'll just drive." Theresa hit him in the arm gently, playfully, and leaned over to grab a Lucinda Williams tape out of her purse.

"Were you drowning?" Joe asked.

"What?"

"In your dream, were you drowning?"

"No," Theresa said thoughtfully, "I was transforming."

"Into what?"

"I don't know, something better, I think. Something less bound."

"All my dreams are nightmares," Joe said only half jokingly.

"You've got to learn how to dream right, baby," Theresa replied. "You know that book I've been reading about the desert around the Salton Sea?"

"Yeah."

"It says that the Indians who lived out there believed that you dreamed your spirit, your whole identity, in the womb before you were born. Your entire life afterward was a process of remembering, trying to get back to a more perfect state."

"Becoming whole," Joe said as he glanced over at an Indian casino by the side of freeway.

"Right," Theresa continued, "You were judged by your dreams, too. Not just the dreams but how you told them."

"A visionary culture," Joe said as they left the last vestiges of the easternmost suburbs of the city behind.

"People who knew how to dream," Theresa said glancing out the window at the sign for Highway 79. As Joe pulled off the freeway and turned left toward the Cuyamacas, she remembered her sister's crack about how she should have found a "full-time professor," but she didn't care. Joe had been so nice with Cecilia when they met for the first time last week. He was a good one, she thought. It had been her idea to go out to Borrego for a day or two. She loved the desert; everything fell away there.

They listened to a song about driving through the country as they weaved their way along the winding road into the forest. The mid-afternoon sun filtered through the oaks and pines, leaving intricate patterns of shadows on the road. Theresa caught a glimpse of a deer in a distant grove. When Joe slowed down to look, the woman in the sports car behind them leaned on her horn and sped recklessly around their car, risking a head-on collision with an equally hurried pickup truck coming from the other direction.

"That blessed mood," Joe said ironically.

"What?" Theresa asked.

"It's Wordsworth," Joe said. "Commenting on the transformative power of nature."

"Which poem?"

"Tintern Abbey." They drove out of the forest and emerged into a large meadow, where Joe spotted a hawk circling. There were horseback riders in the distance and the sky was a clean light blue. Lucinda was singing about love, pain, and memory as they reached Cuyamaca Lake, passed by a roadhouse for fishermen and day travelers, and looked at the little boats bobbing on the cobalt blue water.

"Do you want to stop in Julian?" Theresa asked.

"No, I'm not feeling theme-park enough," Joe replied.

"Okay, Mr. Intellectual, no pie for you," Theresa said mockingly.

"That's fine with me," he said with a chuckle.

They cruised into the edge of Julian and the cars were lined up all the way to the end of the street. Joe could see the signs for homemade everything and the crowd of people walking impatiently down the overcrowded Disney-like main street. There was even a horse-drawn carriage being trailed by a Mazda yearning for the open road.

"It's not that bad," Theresa insisted. "On the far side there's a cool old cemetery, and the road goes out toward some nice farms."

"It's just the mandatory 'family' nature of the place," Joe said. "You've got to be in the mood."

"I know what you mean," Theresa agreed. "We can skip it." Joe turned off of Highway 79 onto 78, and they headed down the mountain by Whispering Pines, Banner, and Scissor's Crossing toward the desert. As they descended, the temperature rose steadily and the landscape gradually shifted, pines giving way to cacti and ocotillo; green grasses and yellow flowers replaced by tawny boulders and light sand. Something about the mesmerizing twists and turns of the road and the growing starkness of the land made them silent. By the time Joe crossed Highway S2, it was well over ninety degrees. He glanced over at Theresa wiping the sweat off her brow with her hand and felt his head lighten from the change in temperature. There was a dead snake on the side of the road and the asphalt was glowing in the distance. At certain points, the big rocks looked artfully stacked, arranged like a mammoth Zen garden, beautifully spare. But there was no intention, no purpose. Joe's mind sifted through memories of images from John Ford's old western *Stagecoach*, Wim Wenders' film *Paris, Texas,* and a black-and-white still photograph of a desert road in the fifties by Robert Frank. He thought about *On the Road, The Grapes of Wrath,* and the Bible, pondered the mute ancient stones, and surrendered himself to the utter strangeness of it all. When they turned onto S3, he was struck by the notion that he was on a pilgrimage of sorts, that something was going to happen. He smiled at his idea, but somehow it stuck with him. Slowly a few structures appeared in the distance as they approached Borrego Springs, the small town in the middle of the Anza-Borrego State Park.

"When I first came out here, I couldn't get over this place," Joe said, at last breaking the silence. "Coming from Ohio, it was like visiting the moon."

"Everywhere looks like the moon compared to Ohio," Theresa said teasingly.

"Very funny," Joe shot back feigning insult. They rolled by a few lonely ranch houses, a dead motel, a fancy "planned community" named Ram's Hill, and Casa del Zorro, a Mission-style resort, before arriving at Christmas Circle and swinging around the roundabout that encompassed a small park across from a smattering of closed date stands, after which came the main street. Joe was glad to see that the bar and the taco place were still open, even in June.

"It's just a little past the bar," Theresa said, directing him to the motel she'd reserved for the night. Joe saw a kitschy sign with a big orange sun, pulled into the driveway of the House of the Sun, and stopped the car.

"I'll take care of it," Theresa said as she got out of the car. Joe watched her walk into the lobby and noticed the sweat running down her back under her thin white blouse. The seat marks on the backs of her legs filled him with affection. It was all good, he thought, everything was easy with her. He saw the man behind the desk beaming as he spoke to her. When she came out, they drove the car down a short sand path past a row of empty rooms to an isolated duplex. It seemed like they were the only people there.

"These are great," Joe said, noticing the view of the open desert behind the room and the Chocolate Mountains in the distance.

"It's like our own little house," Theresa said, "and at the extreme heat-wave discount." They grabbed their bags and headed into the room. It was stifling, so Theresa immediately turned the air conditioner on high. Joe noted the sixties-style decor appreciatively and glanced at the green grape vine hand-stenciled on the cream-colored cinderblock wall. He walked out of the front room and passed through the bedroom into the small kitchen to put the fruit they'd brought into the fridge. Theresa came in behind him with a bottle of vodka and some bubbly water.

"Let's make drinks and go swimming," she said.

"Great idea," Joe answered, looking approvingly at the bottle of Absolut.

"Which, the drink or the swim?" Theresa said, and laughed.

"Both," Joe said, grabbing an ice tray out of the freezer and proceeding to mix their drinks in two big plastic cups. While he was pouring, Theresa stripped off her sweaty clothes and searched through her bag for her one-piece bathing suit. Joe came into the room with the drinks, put them down on the bedside table, and embraced her from behind, burying his face in the moist curve of her neck.

"Not until the AC's been on for a while, okay, honey?" Theresa said as she turned and kissed him. "Now give me my drink and put your suit on." Joe stripped down as well and found his trunks in his bag.

"I forgot to bring a book," he said mournfully.

"You can read mine while I swim," Theresa said after taking the first sip of her drink. "This is good, very cool."

They walked out into the blazing sun and found the pool in the middle of the circle of duplexes. There was nobody there.

"This is perfect," Theresa said as she set her cup down, dropped her towel on a lounge chair in the shade under the awning, and jumped into the pool feet first.

Joe watched her sink to the bottom and pop back up to the surface. He sat down on the lounge chair next to hers, took a sip of his drink, and watched her rearrange her hair.

"In real life you come back up," he said. "In dreams it's easy."

"Dreams are real."

"What do you think yours meant?"

"That I want to die. At some level I want to let go of myself."

"Suicide?"

"No, I want to let one self die so another can be born."

"What's the old self?"

"The part that's afraid," she said paddling over to sit down on the bottom step, leaving all but her head still submerged in the water.

"Afraid of what?"

"The world. When you've been messed up like I've been, you get scared in a big way. Even when there's nothing to be scared of anymore."

"You mean your ex-husband?"

"Mostly yes, I guess, but it also has to do with having a child. The world can seem like it's full of menace and danger and you forget joy."

"Doesn't Cecilia bring you joy?"

"She does, but with that kind of love you also get worry, deep worry. For years I was so lost in it that I forgot myself."

"You've never told me this before."

"You only know me on my days off, honey. Besides, it's not sexy." Theresa smiled wryly at this admission and stared at Joe probingly.

"It doesn't matter," he said gently, seriously.

"We'll see how it is after you get used to having regular sex," she said with a playfully evil grin.

"How do you know I wasn't having regular sex before?" he said, putting his drink down and wading in to the pool to hug her.

"A woman can sense these things. Besides, your shirts were always wrinkled." They both laughed at this, and Joe ducked his head, popped back up and said, "So who's the new self?"

"We'll see," she said, diving under the water and swimming across the pool into the sunny end where she hopped out and sat on the edge, dangling her feet in the water daintily, putting her head back to soak up some sun. Joe got out of the pool and lay back on the lounge in the shade. He took a sip of his drink and picked up Theresa's book about the Salton Sea. He leafed through the section about the local Indians and thought about what Theresa had said about letting yourself die. Maybe that had been his father's problem, clinging bitterly to a failed self. He thought about his mother and resolved to call her next week. Across the pool, Theresa was still baking in the late afternoon sun. It must have been 5:00 or so, but it felt like noon, or some other time outside of time. Joe read a section on William Blake, the geologist who first charted the region in the middle of the nineteenth century and described the Indians as Arabs. He flipped through another section about the business scams pulled by the water barons whose haphazard scheme to divert the Colorado River for irrigation resulted in the disastrous floods that created the Salton Sea at the turn of the century.

Theresa jumped back into the pool and a lizard scurried by his plastic cup on the ground. Joe dove back into the book and read that 9000 acres of land under the Salton Sea was granted to the Torres-Martinez Band of Desert Cahuilla Indians in 1909. They were still waiting for it to dry up. He skimmed a chapter on farm labor and gazed at a photo of a farm worker leaning proudly on a hoe, his tired eyes staring sternly into the camera, the crop rows rolling on forever behind him. His expression, Joe thought, was beautifully defiant. In another chapter, he read about M. Penn Phillips who, in the late fifties, marketed real estate by the sea, which he dubbed "the Salton Riviera," the great resort city of the future. "Now our dream is coming to life," he told the thousands of working stiffs who bought his line about a low-rent Palm Springs by a desert oasis. Joe glanced at a picture of dead fish washed up on the beach and another of the broken ruins of the Salton City Yacht Club. When the sea started to rot, Mr. Phillips retired a wealthy man and left it to others to discover that rain doesn't always follow the bulldozer. Toward the end of the book, Joe looked at some photos of Slab City, a camp for impoverished snowbirds near a bombing range. It was like another world, forgotten by history. The whole thing fascinated him.

"Let's drive around the Sea tomorrow," he said to Theresa as she emerged from the pool, dripping wet.

"Okay, but I'm warning you, it's smelly."

"The smellier the better," he replied with mock enthusiasm.

"It's a trip, you'll like it," Theresa said as she lay back on the lounge and took a sip of her drink. Joe put down the book and watched the sun slowly sinking behind the mountains. He closed his eyes after the glare became too intense, seeing bright white dots on the backs of his eyelids. He turned on his side, opened his eyes, and gazed at Theresa, lying beside him with her eyes closed. She had never seemed so beautiful to him as she did today, and it made him vaguely uneasy. What she had said about her life had unmoored his previous image of her from its foundations and changed his whole story. She was more fragile now, and that made him feel vulnerable. He wondered how she saw him, wondered about his own narrative about himself. We are the intricate web of the stories we tell ourselves, he thought—all the lies, hopes, and dreams. He told himself that the connection he felt to her was truer and stronger than any of their differences. He told himself that he would not lie, try not to lie, to this woman, but he didn't know if that was possible. The thought that what he perceived as his greatest truths might be nothing more than convenient, transitory stories chilled him a little.

Theresa opened her eyes and smiled at him. She took a sip of her now-lukewarm drink and tossed the rest out.

"Let's go inside," she said. They picked up their things and strolled out of the pool area, down a little path by a cactus garden toward their duplex. It looked like nobody else had checked in. About ten feet from their door, Theresa stopped in her tracks and grabbed Joe's hand, pulling his attention away from the horizon.

A roadrunner had stopped right in front of them, and stood there, frozen for a few seconds before darting away.

"I'd never seen one," she said. "I always wonder what the consciousness of animals is like. I wonder, did that bird see me the way I saw it?"

"You know what a scientist would tell you?" Joe said, as Theresa opened the front door to find the room refreshingly cool.

"I don't care."

"Neither do I," Joe said. Theresa took off her suit and got in the shower. Joe felt his desire rise as he watched her walk into the bathroom, so he stripped off his trunks, followed her in, and stepped behind the curtain.

"Well, hello," she said. They kissed and washed each other caressingly, stumbled out of the shower and started to make love on the floor at the foot of the bed. When he entered her, Joe was surprised by her welcoming heat, and had to slow down to keep from spending himself. She recognized this and it excited her.

"Slow," she whispered in a voice that hit his ear like honey. After a while, he found a good rhythm and Theresa came quickly, moaning heavily and squeezing her legs around his waist hard. When he finished, it was so intense he could feel it from the base of his spine all the way up his back. The anxiety of unknowing he had felt by the pool had stayed with him and made their love making more intense, like a trading of trembling souls.

"You fit me," Theresa said in the same sweet whisper, still lying beneath him. They got up and rinsed off again briefly and came back out without dressing.

"Hey, I've got a surprise," Theresa said opening her hand to expose a small white capsule.

"What is it?"

"It's X."

"Ecstasy?"

"Yeah, let's do it tonight."

"I've heard it gives you a wicked hangover."

"This stuff is clean. I haven't done it, but I got it from a friend that I trust. Don't worry." Theresa swallowed hers and looked at Joe coyly as she passed him a cup of water. He looked at the capsule, put it in his mouth, and took a swig of water.

"It'll take a while to come on. First you'll feel a little speedy, but then it eases in nicely."

"I hope so."

"I've gotta pee, I'll be right back," Theresa said before disappearing into the other room. Joe tried to relax and flipped on the TV. It was CNN. First there was a story about environmental problems in Ecuador's Amazonian region. U.S. oil companies had left hundreds of exposed toxic pits that were killing off whole tribes and threatening endangered species. After that came the medical report. There was a new breast cancer treatment, and it was showing mixed results. Joe was just about to change the channel when it switched to a story about the club drug Ecstasy that, according to a new study, depletes the brain of serotonin. Short- and long-term effects were said to include depression, psychosis, and, in a few isolated cases, death. Researchers had studied rave goers in Europe who frequently did the drug and determined that long-term use might result in very serious consequences. Joe was just starting to feel a little jittery when he heard Theresa's voice behind him.

"Hey, turn that thing off. Remember what I said about the nightmare machine?"

"Did you hear what it said?"

"We're not 'frequent users,' honey. I've known the girl I got this from since high school. She wouldn't give me bad stuff. She's Catholic." Theresa giggled after the last remark, and Joe smiled.

"But seriously," she continued, "I think taking in all that shit on

TV and the radio is bad for your soul, you know? It takes you away from yourself."

"I know what you mean, and sometimes it can do that, but the way I see it, you can't shut the world out and be whole. You need to find your place in it, its place in you."

"And all that ugliness helps you how?"

"Sometimes you've got to know gutter water to truly taste wine."

"It's too much, Joe, you can't take it all in or there'll be nothing left of you. You'll find yourself in the gutter plenty of times without going and looking for it. But maybe that's just because I've known a little bit more of it than you, I think. You white boys have it a little easier sometimes," she said teasingly, but seriously.

"Maybe so," Joe admitted, feeling a new tightness in his chest. "Today, while we were lying by the pool, I wondered about that."

"About what?"

"About what we really know about each other, about what I know about myself, about anything. After all, who's to say that we really even have a 'self' to be true to? Maybe we just make the whole thing up."

"What do you think?"

"I don't know. Sometimes I feel full, sometimes I feel empty. Since we've been seeing each other I've felt full of life, full of love, certain, but who's to say it will last? Maybe all we get are fleeting moments and then it's back to the emptiness. Maybe there's really just nothing at the core of it all. And everything else is just bullshit."

"That's pretty grim, but sometimes I think the same thing."

"But other times I suspect that the grim truth is too easy."

"Do you believe in God?"

"I don't know. If there is a God, I think it's everything from the dirt to the stars. What we can see and touch and what we can't. If not, we're all we have, but that's not necessarily so bad. It's a hard thought to think that it's just you alone in the world with nothing to fall back on but yourself, but there's a beauty to that as well. We make our lives, struggle to become something."

"Maybe," Theresa interjected, "it's both. We swing between fullness and emptiness and couldn't know one without the other. All I know is that I feel full with you." She smiled and kissed him and the touch of her lips melted into Joe's face.

"I think I feel something," he said.

"Me too. Just go with it," she said running her hands through his hair and down his neck to his chest. Joe leaned over and sucked on one of her nipples and it felt good, but she felt sensual in a way that was more oceanic than focused. She touched his cheek and guided his face up toward hers.

"Tell me your heart," she whispered.

"I love you," he said.

"Are you in for the long haul?" she said gazing deeply into his sleepy green eyes.

"I'm in," he said. Theresa kissed him long and hard, not knowing where she stopped and he began. Joe felt himself swimming in the ocean of her hair, smelling it as he had never smelled anything. He felt deeper inside the moment than he ever had. It was as if someone had cracked open the shell of a second and it had spilled out and enveloped them. When they stopped kissing, he noticed that the edges had come off the world. He felt a fluid connection between their bodies and even the couch they were sitting on and the air flowing in and out of their lungs. Without speaking, he took Theresa's hand and they walked into the kitchen. He poured some water into a cup and they shared it, feeling like it was the very nectar of life. Joe grabbed an apple out of the fridge and handed it to her.

"Isn't that my job?" Theresa said at last, laughing.

"We're not gonna fall," Joe said, smiling before taking a bite out of the apple and noticing every bit of its texture, every nuance of its rich sweetness. Then he turned off the light, opened the back door, and they stepped naked out into the night. The air was like velvet on their skin, and everything between the warm sand and the myriad stars was surging with being, singing the sweet song of the cosmos.

✦ ✦ ✦

Joe woke up the next morning when the sun crept through the blinds. He was pleased to discover that he didn't feel bad. Theresa stirred slowly beside him and opened her eyes to see Joe's face next to hers, staring at her.

"You know all that stuff I said last night on drugs?"

"Yeah, they were sweet," she said sleepily.

"I was just kidding," he said grinning devilishly.

"I see you're not dead," she said as she pushed his head away playfully when he tried to kiss her. "Make me some coffee, funny man."

Joe got up, walked into the kitchen and put the kettle on. His senses were normal again, but slightly heightened. The coffee smell, the oranges, the morning air out the back door were all still nicely vivid. He heard the sound of the shower and went back into the bedroom to leave Theresa's coffee on the nightstand. Today they were going to drive out to look at the Badlands and then loop around the Sea. He went over the plan in his head, sipping his coffee, relishing seeing some places he'd never been to. He felt like a kid on Christmas. Once Theresa was done, he hopped in the shower and after that they headed out, stopping first for a machaca burrito to bolster the fruit.

"Are you okay?" Joe asked as the parked in front of the stand.

"Yeah, why?"

"You're quiet. That's all."

"We said enough last night. I'm happy. Just a little tired still. It's hot."

"Okay, just checking." She patted his shoulder and they walked into the furnace-like storefront for the burritos. It was probably already over 90 degrees, even at 9:00 A.M. The woman behind the counter took their order without speaking. When the food was ready, they ate it silently, chewing and sweating over a little red table. Outside the air was not much better, so Joe ran into the liquor store to buy several bottles of water for the drive.

Once they were on the road, the breeze and motion made things far more tolerable.

"I'll think of it like a vision quest," Theresa said jokingly. After a few miles, Joe saw the marker for Font's Point Wash and turned off onto the sand. The car rattled along adequately for a bit before almost getting stuck in the sand. Joe adjusted in time and kept going for about a mile until they hit the end of the road. When he parked the car, they still couldn't see anything. After they hiked up a small hill to the bluff, however, the view of the Badlands was breathtaking. Joe scanned the labyrinth of multihued hills and gorges, a mosaic of green, yellow, pink, and red. He spotted a hawk circling overhead and felt the hot wind rising up off of the ancient desert. Time stops here, he thought, enjoying the feeling again.

"Have a vision yet?" he asked Theresa.

"It's sacred without a church," she said thoughtfully.

"Like the very house of stillness," he said.

"Baked stillness," she said as she pulled her hair back into a ponytail. They returned to the car, drove halfway back to the road, and stopped at a marker for petroglyphs. Joe pulled over, and they got out again and hiked for about a quarter of a mile before they found some barely visible geometric shapes. Theresa walked over to the rock and stared hard at the shapes. Somebody had scratched "Ron was here" next to the markings.

"Before/After," Joe said wryly.

"It's a shame, they'll just vanish into time soon. Nobody's even sure what they meant."

"There's something nice about that, though," Joe said. Theresa didn't reply, sighing instead and turning back toward the car.

Back on the road, Theresa sucked down half a bottle of water and passed the rest to Joe. He took the bottle, finished it quickly, and checked the temperature gauge—still okay. It seemed he was sweating a lot more today. He looked over at Theresa who was staring blankly into the distance.

"How are you, really?" he asked.

"A little flat," she said. "I'll live." Joe touched her arm and noticed it was wet with sweat. Suddenly, inexplicably, he was hit by a wave of sadness. He gazed ahead at the empty highway and felt as if he was going to weep. He noticed a dead coyote by the shoulder of the road, pondered the cloudless sky, and thought about the whiteness of the whale chapter in *Moby Dick*, the colorless nothing that lies beneath the surface world of colors. Last night it was full; today it was empty. A rabbit dashed across the road in front of the car, barely escaping with its life. It was several more miles before they hit Salton City. Joe thought about the geologist, William Blake, who surveyed this region on a mule with very little water, jotting down notes about the rock formations.

"How hot do you think it is?" he asked Theresa.

"One hundred," she offered.

"One hundred and five," Joe guessed, upping the ante. It was hard to say if the blasting wind made things better, but he didn't have air conditioning. Another rabbit raced across the road, surviving the gamble, making Joe glad not to be the angel of its death. In some strange way, the harshness of the heat combined with the dead, burned landscape grounded him. There was a purity to it. Joe was going eighty-five miles an hour. He noticed a tear rolling down

Theresa's cheek, took one hand off of the wheel, and gently wiped it away.

"The desert blooms in the spring," he said.

"I know," she answered, thinking of the time she'd come out here with Cecilia to camp one April. Cecelia had learned the names of the flowers and walked down the trail to the Palm Oasis reciting them: verbena, desert paintbrush, woolly daisy, ghost flower. "Ghost flowers," Theresa said.

Joe saw the sign for Salton City and a few buildings appeared on the outskirts in the near distance: a dumpy little house that looked abandoned, a government building of some kind, the shell of a dead motel: the Sundowner. He came to a stop at Highway 86 and looked both ways. There was no traffic. As he crossed the highway and pulled into the town, Joe noticed a closed restaurant and a gas station with nobody there but the attendant. He turned down a road that looked like it went toward the water and saw how the desolate, empty lots were dotted with a number of small houses, some that seemed occupied, some not. They drove by a place with an old Ford pickup and a broken-down dune buggy parked in the gravel driveway in front of a faded brown garage. There was an elderly Mexican woman hanging a white dress on a line by the side of the house, she waved. The windows of her house were all shaded, one of them with a piece of cardboard that said, "Happy Birthday Jesus." The empty lots that surrounded the house were littered with scraps of lumber, car batteries, rusty dirt-bike parts, and an odd mishmash of other detritus.

After a bit, they came upon a dead motel from the late fifties, the front of each room decorated by either a sea horse or a marlin. A man in a safari hat and a Finland T-shirt was snapping pictures of the empty pool and looked up nervously as they rolled by him slowly. Joe glanced over at another house that had a black van in the driveway with a big American flag painted on the side. The front of the shabby yellow bungalow was adorned with a rock garden where the owner had placed a hand-drawn sign that said "U.S. out of the U.N." Past a few more empty lots, Theresa nudged him and pointed to a house that looked deserted at first, until Joe noticed the Harley leaning against the side of the house. There was a dying tree out back, and under it sat a scrawny, shirtless man with long gray hair, a thick beard, and a fading mandala tattoo that covered his entire torso. He was sitting on a beach chair, staring at them blankly. It looked like he was shooting up. Joe drove by more empty lots and then a row of better kept little ranch houses that had battered campers in the driveway sporting bumper stickers that said "Snowbird," "Over Sixty but Still Sexy," and "We're Spending Our Children's Inheritance." After a while he came to another road that clearly lead to the Sea, turned right, and cruised toward the shimmering water.

"This must be the way to the old Yacht Club," he said.

"Wonderful, let's stop for a cocktail," Theresa joked as they drove past a row of dead palm trees that led to the water's edge, the stench rising steadily the closer they got. Joe tried to block the smell out and imagine this place through the eyes of the boosters of the "Salton Riviera." He fancied the shore covered with beach towels, where tourists sat sipping tropical drinks, observing the waterskiers frolicking on the open sea, the fishermen hauling in big corvinas. As Joe approached the water's edge, he saw the foundation of what must have been the ruins of the Yacht Club. Joe stopped the car and they got out to survey the scene. It looked as though it had burned down. The charred wreckage was surrounded by a chain-link fence. Outside the car, the smell of the rotting sea was even more powerful. Joe and Theresa walked along the fence until they came to a patch of open beach, blanketed with the decaying corpses of fish. The water was a thick, syrupy, brackish green, and they could see a few fish swimming lethargically near the surface, waiting to suffocate in the algae bloom. Joe picked up a big rock and hurled it into the sea, creating a sluggish splash of water and other viscous matter.

"It's like a beach in hell," Theresa observed.

"Or vacationing after the apocalypse," Joe agreed. They turned around and got back into the car. Joe tried to take a different way back and got lost, zigzagging his way through a totally empty stretch. He saw a sign for a golf course and went the other way, passing through a series of vacant lots. The sun had burned the names off the street signs and people had used them for target practice. Joe turned onto another street with a few more houses on it. There was a tiny blue ranch house with a "For Sale" sign posted in the yard: $3,000. After a few more empty lots, they came upon a short row of pale gray boxes. One of the houses had a covered patio, and Joe saw a whole family sitting around a picnic table in the shade, eating. The truck in the driveway had a UFW sticker on the bumper. An elderly neighbor was making his way over with what looked like cake. Joe made another turn and passed by several open lots littered with garbage and then an isolated place surrounded by a huge, artfully done cactus garden. In the lot next to the cactus garden there was a half-constructed sculpture of something made out of random junk. Next to it sat another finished piece, an awkward heart shape, about six feet high, put together with various auto parts and chicken wire, the screen of a dead TV at its center. The whole scene filled Joe with a bittersweet melancholy. He savored it. This is where you go when you stop wanting, he thought. Occupy the wreckage of a dead dream. If the world pushes you too hard, just stop pushing back.

"It's outside of time," he said out loud at last. "You've got to give the place that. Less than a hundred miles away time and space are crashing in on everyone, strangling them. Here the world is definitely not too much with you."

"It's so depressing," she replied. "How could it be good to live next door to an environmental disaster?"

"The mind is its own place," Joe said. "All I'm saying is that maybe some of these people came here to escape. If it was Palm Springs, it wouldn't be the same. You'd have to have money, you'd have to have responsibilities, you'd have to be part of everything. Nobody expects anything of you after the apocalypse."

"I could see what you're saying if it wasn't so stinky," Theresa said holding her nose goofily as she spoke, then laughing. Joe laughed too and was glad to see her smile.

"So you're feeling better," he asked as he finally found his way out of a vacant patch and came to the road they drove in on.

"I was never that bad. I just feel raw. Everything is a bit more intense, that's all. My friend said that's a pretty normal thing the day after."

"I feel the same way—edgy but not bad," Joe said. As they approached the intersection where they entered, Theresa noticed what looked like a bar down the road by the gas station with several cars in front of it.

"Let's go in there and get a drink with some ice in it," she said. Joe turned left at the intersection and pulled up in front of a dingy little place: The 10th Boardroom, Cocktails and Mini-mart.

"Maybe we can get some more water, too. We only have three bottles left, and we might need more," he said, as he surveyed the little patio in back where a woman in a baggy blue dress and a white apron was stirring something in a big metal pot.

"Good idea." They walked past a beat-up Dodge Dart, a forlorn dune buggy, and a golf cart and headed in, feeling the heat seep through the soles of their shoes as they walked. Inside, it took a while for their eyes to adjust to the dark. Slowly, Joe saw a paltry assortment of canned goods on a shelf to their right, no water. This must be the mini-mart, he thought. He looked left and noticed a row of grungy old men with cowboy hats and thick beards looking at him. He nodded, and one of them said, "Howdy."

"Hi," Theresa replied. They walked by the old guys, who were wearing dirty undershirts and drinking Pabst in the can, and then strolled past a long table next to the bar. It was ringed with patrons of various stripes. Joe glanced at a large elderly woman, who looked Asian, in a pink and yellow polka-dot summer dress sipping a glass of water. She was sitting beside a very old man, maybe in his nineties, so drunk that the woman periodically had to steady him to keep him from falling off of his stool. He slurred something incomprehensible to Joe, who leaned forward only to hear a woman's voice behind him saying, "Don't bother, honey. Drunk and no dentures is a bad combination." Joe turned to see the stout figure of the bartender, a sweet-faced middle-aged Latina.

"What can I get for you two?" she asked.

"A Coke with ice," Theresa said.

"Two," Joe added. The bartender walked over to the freezer to grab the Cokes, and Joe turned back around to look at the rest of the customers circling the table. Next to the drunk old man, he saw a guy who looked just like Harry Dean Stanton in *Paris, Texas,* hollow-eyed and lonely, deep lines etched into his face. He was sitting by another man who was wearing a down vest, no shirt beneath it. The man in the vest was also wearing a faded orange cap with a golf-ball patch on the front. "Meet me at the 19th hole," it read. Behind the two men, Joe saw another table against the far wall where two middle-aged couples, all in Hawaiian shirts, sat playing some kind of card game, sipping on long neck Buds.

"Here you go, my dear," the bartender said regaining Joe's attention. "We're cooking up some hobo stew out back if you guys are hungry."

"Thanks, but we ate," Joe said.

"It's good stew," she insisted, smiling broadly, exposing a gold tooth. "Everybody brings a can of something and we throw it all together. This time it came out good."

"Thanks, we really did eat, though," Joe said, feeling a bit ungenerous.

"Okay, honey. You don't have to eat our soup," she teased him. "One dollar." Joe paid, reaching over the shoulder of a man in overalls with no shirt beneath.

"Where you two hail from?" he asked with a thick southern accent as he turned around, grinned, and adjusted his red and white ball cap with a fish on the front. Joe looked at his handlebar mustache. There was a scar under his left eye.

"San Diego," Theresa said.

"Watcha here for?" he asked, nodding to her.

"To look at the old Yacht Club, but it's gone," Joe said.

"Burnt down," he explained.

"Homeless," the bartender interjected, motioning toward the cowboy hats near the door. "It gets cold at night in the winter."

"Just as well without it, piece of junk," said the man.

"Made this place look like a dump," agreed the bartender.

"Thanks," Joe said nodding to them as Theresa tapped his arm to come find a seat. They walked by the pool table toward an empty seat next to the air conditioner. A woman in cut-offs and a Tahiti tank top walked over and put some quarters in the jukebox, and the Texas Tornados came on. Joe noticed that the guy they had seen taking pictures of the motel was playing pool with another guy in a polo shirt, J. Crew shorts, and tasseled loafers. He didn't fit in. Joe overheard the well-dressed man telling his pool opponent that he was here with some company to "study desalinization strategies." It made Joe think of M. Penn Phillips, dreaming of the Salton Riviera.

"It's like the party for the end of the world," Theresa said as she watched a woman walk in and be greeted by the whole bar. "But they're kind to each other." They watched the bartender go out the back door and come back in bit later.

"Soup's on!" she yelled cheerfully and then, as she passed their table, "You sure you don't want some stew? Take a bowl if you want."

"Thank you," Theresa said. Slowly, one by one, everyone in the bar but the guy in the polo shirt got up to get some stew. The homeless men went back for seconds. People held the door for each other and complimented the bartender on her cooking. The bartender came over and handed them bowls. Theresa found the gesture so moving she teared-up a little. She wiped her eyes and headed outside. One of the homeless men held the door for her. While she was outside, Joe noticed some pictures pinned to a bulletin board on the wall near their table. The same people in the same bar at Halloween, Christmas, Easter, and Thanksgiving. Theresa came back in with a tiny bowl of stew.

"It's terrible," she said as she took a few bites. Joe smiled and patted her hand as she made herself finish it. Patsy Cline came on, "Crazy," and Joe watched an elderly couple get up to dance. There was something painfully fragile and, at the same time, graceful about the way they held each other. When the song was over, people clapped.

"We better go," he said to Theresa who was watching them as well.

"Back into the world," she said wistfully. The bartender yelled, "Thank you!" as they headed out the door, and one of the homeless cowboys said, "Take care of yourselves, now." Outside, the midday heat was still excruciating. One hundred and ten, Joe guessed. They got back into the car and drove to the highway.

"It was like a communion," Theresa said thoughtfully. Joe nodded silently as they came to a halt at Highway 86.

"Do you mind if we stop and look at this old motel for a second?" he asked.

"No, go ahead."

Joe crossed the highway and parked the car in front of the ruins of the Sundowner Motel. They got out and looked at the Texas Barbeque sign still hanging in the last surviving window of the ghostly Roadrunner lounge. Joe led them toward the area where the rooms had been, kicking an old wheel from a rollaway bed, glancing down at a door from a blackened freezer, a box spring, and the shell of an air conditioner.

"Hey, look," said Theresa, pointing to an unsoiled page from a porno magazine, a picture of two buxom blond women in a banal, calculated embrace against a lurid red backdrop. Next to the picture was a copy of the want ads from the *Los Angeles Times*. Joe leaned over and picked up the paper. It was from January of 1998, and someone had circled an ad that called for "winners with attitude" to do telemarketing. They strolled over to the pool area where the "No Lifeguard" sign was still looming on a post. Joe kicked a broken porcelain fixture and stared at some remaining iron stairs, leading upward into nothing. They turned around and walked back to the car quietly, hopped in, and drove toward Valerie Jean.

Joe hit the accelerator and the car slowly climbed up past sixty to seventy and began to strain near eighty. He slowed down and settled in at seventy and the temperature gauge evened out. Theresa opened another bottle of water, drank gratefully, and passed it over to Joe. She put sunscreen on her left arm and glanced over at the sparkling illusion of the distant water as they passed by Salton Sea Beach.

"It's gorgeous when you can't smell it," she said. Joe nodded as a big rig roared by them on the other side of the road. They sped past a sign for a motor-home park advertising "Corvina Beach: A

Fisherman's Paradise." Near Desert Shores, another fading sign welcomed sportsmen and had a picture of water-skiers. Joe watched a motor home straight out of *Road Warrior* turn left in front of him and drive into Desert Shores. Something about the speed of driving made them want music. Theresa put one of Joe's John Coltrane tapes in, and "Giant Steps" came on. The intricate beauty of the piece was utterly disconcerting in contrast to the corpses of road-houses that lined the highway. Joe tapped the steering wheel to the beat, and a feeling of euphoria began to build in him as he gazed at the double yellow line in the middle of the road, stared back at the empty highway in his rearview mirror. Theresa put her hand on the back of his neck and it felt hot, but nice. As they came to the Riverside–San Diego County line, the light-colored limestone of Travertine Rock appeared on their left, sporting a multitude of huge trivial inscriptions. Joe thought he saw "Mike Rules" near the top. William Blake had come upon this as well, he remembered. They passed by a sign for the Indian Reservation, and evidence of agriculture started to emerge. There was a grove of palm trees in the distance, and Theresa squeezed the back of his neck.

"Let's stop for a date shake," she said, "I'll show you where." Joe noticed a few more trucks on the highway as they approached the grove, and Theresa pointed to a little shack in the midst of the palm trees adorned with handwritten signs advertising various date products. Joe pulled over and they got out and walked in.

"I came here once as a kid," she told him on the way in. Theresa ordered two date shakes from a bored teenage girl behind the counter. Joe walked outside to the car, grabbed his notebook, and headed over to the little patio under the palms while Theresa waited for the shakes. He sat down on little stool made out of a crate next to a circular table that consisted of a piece of plywood nailed to a barrel. The shade felt nice, and the sun seemed less brutal filtered through the trees. He looked down at his notebook and jotted down a few details from their trip: the house with the heart sculpture, the name of the bar, the want ads in the rubble of the Sundowner Motel. Then he stopped and wrote a line: *This much I know about desire*. He was just about to pen another line, when he noticed Theresa behind him with the shakes. She handed him one and sat down on a crate next to him.

"Do you ever feel like you're living your life in order to write about it? In order to have something to say?" she said probingly.

"It's more like I'm chasing ghosts. Trying to hold on to the substance and meaning of a moment as it fades away," he replied.

"But how do you know that you are really in the moment or if you're just framing your life for a picture you'll paint later? Maybe you're just stuck in your head."

"You have to try to be honest."

"And you think you can be honest about that?" Theresa said, smiling as she took her first sip of date shake, puckering her mouth in response to the sweetness.

"That's hard to say. I try."

"You do well, I think," she said putting her hand on his leg. "Do you remember that time we read a poem by somebody, Walt Whitman, I think, in class, and that snotty girl asked you if we could leave early?"

"I think so."

"Do you remember what you said?"

"No."

"You said, 'try to be here, in this poem, just for a second.' You said, 'If you give it a chance, it will give you the gift of the moment, make it sacred.'"

"And she rolled her eyes."

"But I listened," Theresa said, kissing him on the cheek. "And I wondered, how do I live? Who am I? Who is this beautiful man? That's when I fell in love with you."

"But you're still not sure whether you know how to occupy the present?" Joe asked with exaggerated incredulity.

"You're not that good," Theresa said teasingly. Joe took a sip of his shake and stuck out his tongue.

"I can't drink this," he said.

"Me either," Theresa said getting up and tossing their shakes in a trashcan behind their table. They got back in the car and drove by more palm groves until they hit Highway 195. A flatbed truck loaded with irrigation pipes labored by on the other side of the road. There were a few fields of other crops that Joe couldn't identify. The smell of earth and chemicals mixed and permeated the hot, dry air. Theresa looked over at a broken-down truck surrounded by farm workers and shook her head. Joe didn't know what time it was and it was, hard to tell. Two o'clock, maybe earlier, maybe later. They came upon 231 and headed through Mecca. It was a farm workers' town without a real main street. Even in the blazing heat, people were out. Joe glanced over at an old woman selling dates by the side of the road. They cruised by some dilapidated looking houses. Norteño blasted out the front door of one house. In another, some kids were splashing around in a blown-up wading pool. Unlike Salton City, this town seemed lived-in, hard-edged. Joe remembered reading there was a lot of heroin out here. He drove by another house where kids were spraying each other with squirt guns and wondered what it was like to grow up here. They drove toward the junction with Highway 111 and saw a large group of migrants hopping in trucks to go out to the fields.

"Es la vida dura," Theresa said, breaking the silence.

"What does that mean," Joe asked.

"It's the hard life," she said.

"I've never heard you speak Spanish before. I didn't know if you could."

"I don't speak much, unfortunately."

174

"Why? Didn't your parents?" Joe asked, as he turned onto Highway 111 and around the back side of the Salton Sea toward North Shore.

"They did, but they wanted us to know English better. They thought it would give us a better life."

"Didn't it?"

"Yes and no. In some ways it made things easier, but in other ways we lost something. I'll never be Anglo, but I'm not totally Mexican either. My grandfather worked out here and organized strikes, but I don't know where or exactly what happened. When we were kids, my sister and I used to tune them out when they told stories. We thought they were boring. But now I feel like I don't know a part of myself, and they're dead and gone."

"A lot of people lose those stories. I don't know anything about my family history."

"I know what you're saying, but it's a little different for me. You're not marked by it like I am," she said seriously.

"I know," Joe said putting one hand on her leg. "Maybe you could learn, ask your parents, do some research."

"Maybe," Theresa said. As they raced by North Shore, there were signs for RV parks and fishing docks. Joe wondered what it would be like to be on a boat in the Sea, fishing for poisoned corvina like some condemned soul floating on the River Styx, forced to eat the gruesome harvest for all of eternity. In the distance, a pelican swooped down from the sky and scooped something out of the water. Joe remembered hearing something on the news about birds dying of an unknown plague. Maybe they could stop at the wildlife refuge after Bombay Beach, he thought, or maybe not. As they drove by the empty state park at Mecca Beach, Joe concluded that this side of the sea seemed even more desolate than the other side.

"Do you think there's a bar in Bombay Beach?" he asked.

"I don't know," Theresa said. "We can check it out, but I don't want to go all the way back tonight after that. Let's see if we can find a place in Brawley with a pool and cool rooms. I'm getting pretty tired of the heat. We can take 8 back home tomorrow, okay?"

"Sure," Joe agreed, just as he saw something smoking on the highway in the distance.

"What's that?" Theresa asked.

"I don't know," Joe said, slowing down and staring ahead. He drove on cautiously, and gradually it became clear what it was, a wreck, and a bad one.

"Oh my God," Theresa said under her breath as they came upon the smoking van and the overturned truck. Joe pulled over and they got out to survey the scene. It appeared that the truck had hit the van head-on and kept going until it had flipped over. The van had been pushed off the road like a crushed can and Joe ran over to find a whole family dead inside. He could see splashes of blood surrounding the horrible collage of flesh and metal pressed into the shattered windshield. A little girl's arm was dangling grotesquely through the broken glass of the passenger-side window.

"Hello!" Joe yelled. Nobody answered. He turned around and ran over to the cab of the truck. It was empty. In back, he found Theresa cradling an old woman in a serape in her arms. The woman was bleeding hard from the head, trying to whisper a word in Spanish. Theresa's white tank top and arms were covered in deep red blood. There were several other motionless bodies that had been flung violently out the back door of the truck. A man in a red flannel shirt whose neck was snapped like dead bird's, another who had flown a few yards farther and shattered his face on the highway. None of it seemed real. Inside the truck, Joe saw several more people, all seemed dead but one, who he found moaning under a pair of legs. He touched the other bodies to feel for breathing. There was none. Everyone looked Mayan, Joe thought. He heard sirens screaming toward them. For some reason, he ran over to grab the last two bottles of water from the car. When he came back, Theresa was weeping silently, staring off into the open desert with a dazed look on her face. The woman in her arms had stopped breathing. Joe went into the truck and held a bottle to the lips of the moaning man; he choked on it and spit it back up. This couldn't be happening, he thought, as he watched the man beneath him dying slowly in the suffocating heat in the back of a cattle truck, how could it?

Dead Motel, Salton City, California

32

He could see the heat rising off the highway in the distance as he drove out of Borrego toward the Salton Sea. It was noon and the temperature was one hundred fifteen and climbing. For a while he drove with the radio off and the AC on, not thinking of anything. The glare was blinding, so he squinted hard and kept driving. There was nobody on the road. The engine strained with the AC on, so he turned it off and opened the window to let the hot air pour in and engulf him. The sudden change made him light-headed, and his body struggled to adjust to the heat. He sweated profusely and stared straight ahead at the hard, barren desert with nothing in bloom. A hawk was circling overhead, and a rabbit dashed across the road. He glanced at his tired blue eyes in the rearview mirror. They didn't seem like his eyes. It was as if they were disembodied somehow, part of himself staring back at himself. Who was behind those eyes? Was it the same thing that saw the hawk and stared at the road? He thought about his desk at the office and his wife and children with immense distance. The most intimate details of his life had no meaning to him. They bored him deeply. He couldn't think of a single thing he felt connected to, not one thing. Maybe the heat would bake this out of him, whatever it was.

He pulled his rented white Ford Escort off the road onto an unmarked wash and drove for a few miles, stirring up dust behind him as he drove. He didn't care where he was going. When the car got stuck in the sand, he got out, locked the door, and walked off into the scorching desert. He could feel the heat of the ground through the soles of his loafers. He listened to the sound of his own footsteps, strangely distant. Sometimes, he thought, if you walked off the side of the road, away from the paths, you found something un-expected. The sweat poured into his eyes and made them sting. He could taste the salt in his mouth. For some reason he was walking quickly, almost rushing. Nobody knows where I am, he thought. He took off his buttoned-down shirt and let the sun burn his pale white skin. Soon he was glistening red, drowning in sweat. The air was so hot it was suffocating. He took deep breaths, but they felt shallow. It was like being underwater. He walked even faster and felt his heart pumping hard, fighting to keep up. Which way was his car? He couldn't see it anymore.

Perhaps he should be afraid, he thought, but he wasn't. His fin-gers felt thick and puffy. He slowed down and focused his gaze on the horizon. How far was it to those mountains? His chest hurt and his heart was racing faster. He sat down to rest on a big rock and the heat burned his skin through his slacks. His heart wouldn't stop racing for a long time, then it did. The thing that he noticed was silence roaring. Was it possible for silence to be loud, deafeningly loud? He lost himself in the howling silence. It was pure, a pure thing. He saw the blue sky, but he didn't see it. He felt the mean sun, but he didn't feel it. It was like being lost at sea. There was some-thing in this, he thought. He wondered how long he had been out here. How long was a second, how long an hour? He suspected time was a false thing. His thirst overwhelmed him like a tidal wave, but he didn't have the energy to get up. He felt drowsy and sick. Every-thing was slipping away from him, slipping away into nothing.

33   There was blood on the nightstand and broken glass on the floor when Alma came in to clean the room. Another one like this and I'll be home late, she thought. It was Marta's tenth birthday and she didn't want to disappoint her. She'd promised tamales and chocolate cake. Alma picked up crushed beer cans, cigarette butts, and a page ripped from a paperback novel with a note scrawled over the text: "Carla, it was hard. I cut my foot bad. There are so many things in this life." Alma wondered who Carla was. She imagined a wife with a kind face full of worry lines, sitting at home, waiting for her drunken husband to return with some lie. Poor woman, she thought, stuck with a bastard. Alma tossed the note in the trash and vacuumed up the broken pieces of a tequila bottle. The fragments of glass rattled violently, but made it into the bag. Good, she didn't want cut fingers. The bed sheets were stained with blood. Alma shook her head in disgust and peeled the soiled linen off the bed, carefully avoiding the red spots. There was a matchbook from the Golden Gate Hotel in Las Vegas on the nightstand next to a book on desert wildflowers. The gambling made sense, but the flowers surprised her. Carla's bastard likes flowers? Alma tried on a different scenario. Maybe it was Carla who left, poor fellow. In the bathroom, there was dried vomit all over the floor. The sympathy poured out of Alma. He was a bastard. She tried to look on the bright side. This job was dirty and the pay was low, but at least they didn't check her papers. The owners were good people. They paid her even when business was slow. Alma got a mop and a bucket and slopped soapy water all over the floor. She didn't like this job, but it could be interesting. There were so many mysteries in other people's messes. Almost everyday she would find something, a piece to the puzzle of a stranger's life.

When she was done, Alma pushed her cart outside of the room into the blazing summer heat, so hot that she melted in it and lost her head. Sometimes when she walked home she would lose a sense of her body. Alma threw away the garbage in a dumpster by the main office, stared off into the desert, and thought about the tourist whose room she'd cleaned a month ago. He'd wandered off into the desert with no water. They never found him, not even a trace. Alma hurried over to the last room for the day wondering what had happened to the lost man who'd left a family behind. What was it like to disappear? Gone, forever. She thought about Marta and her husband and felt afraid. No matter how hard it got, they had each other, she told herself. Alma thought about dying all by herself and it made her feel alone in the world. She bit her lower lip, opened the door to room nine, and got back to work. Tonight, they'd have a nice big dinner, laugh, and be happy. They'd come too far to lose each other. Let the Americans die alone.

34   *The workers were brought in to pick
artichokes, beans, cantaloupes, cauliflower, cucumbers, lettuce,
muskmelons, and more in the brutal heat of the Imperial Valley desert east of San Diego. In temperatures that reached well over one
hundred degrees, Mexican, Japanese, Filipino, East Indian, and
white workers performed the back-breaking labor for little pay, the
non-white majority making a dollar less a day. Mexicans were by far
the largest group, imported since the 1880s as cheap labor by the railroads and the big growers, and by the 1930s they were in the forefront
of the labor struggles. The Sociedad Mutualista Benito Juarez, the
Union of Mexican Field Workers, the Cannery and Agricultural
Workers Industrial Union, and other groups pushed for higher
wages, medical care, and other basic human rights. When they went
on strike, the reaction was ruthless. Police, sheriffs, highway patrol-
men, and vigilantes broke up union meetings in Brawley and El Cen-
tro with tear gas and batons, shut down the pool halls where workers
met in Westmoreland, confiscated union typewriters and mimeo-
graph machines in Azteca Hall, and beat and illegally arrested workers in a prolonged campaign of terrorism. Behind the thugs were the
Imperial Valley Growers and Shippers Protective Association, the
Anti-Communist Association, and the Silver Shirts of San Diego, a
fascist vigilante group.*

*A. L. Wirin, an American Civil Liberties Union lawyer who came
to help the strikers, was kidnapped, severely beaten, robbed, and*

dumped barefoot in the middle of the desert, eleven miles from the town of Calipatria by members of the American Legion. When Brigadier General Pelham Glassford was sent by the United States Secretary of Labor to investigate the situation, he received death threats and was forced to conclude that "a group of growers have exploited a 'communist' hysteria for the advancement of their own interests; they have welcomed labor agitation which they could brand as 'red,' as a means of sustaining supremacy by mob rule, thereby sustaining what is so essential to their profits—cheap labor." But later investigations blamed the presence of communists rather than the inhuman working conditions and obscenely low wages. By the time John Steinbeck's The Grapes of Wrath came out and brought attention to the plight of farm workers, the public face of suffering was white, but despite the attention the novel and movie spurred, little changed.

In the 1960s, César Chávez led a United Farm Workers march from Coachella to Calexico, the workers carrying the black eagle flag of the UFW and a banner of the Virgin of Guadalupe proudly under the scorching sun all the way to the border where Father Victor Salandini held mass for them. The priest, who wore a UFW emblem on his vestments, was chastised by the Bishop of San Diego but loved by the workers. Yet even with the well known efforts of César Chávez from the 1960s on, things are not much better for the worst paid, frequently undocumented workers who in a few notorious cases have actually been forced into slavery. By the 1990 census, twenty-five percent of the Imperial Valley still lived below the poverty line, as some of the last union farms shut down and the companies crossed the border into Mexico chasing cheaper wages and child labor.

35   Joe was sitting by the harbor near the Grape Street Pier, squinting into the dazzling light of the late afternoon sun, watching it dance and shimmer as it spread across the water, infusing the moment with promise. He turned around as a pack of joggers trotted behind him. "Anyone who can't get a job in this market," one of them shouted in between gasps. They were all wearing "running gear," specialized hats, shirts, shorts, and day-glow shoes sporting the latest technological advances. Joe turned his gaze back toward the sun. A sailboat was gliding gracefully on the silvery water. More joggers passed behind him, quietly this time. He listened to their well-cushioned steps recede into the distance and eventually disappear. He felt totally disconnected, out of step, unable even to write.

There had been twenty people inside the truck, the paper had said. They were undocumented workers from southern Mexico and Guatemala. Those who didn't die in the crash ran into the desert to escape, not from *la migra*, but from their captors. The police had found several bodies with gunshot wounds to the back of the head. They never found the driver of the truck, nor his companion. The two survivors told a tale of forced labor on an isolated farm they couldn't identify. Sources revealed that the migrants were being shipped to Los Angeles to work in an athletic shoe factory where counterfeit name brands are produced. "That's how they get treated, as commodities," an INS spokesman had said in the article. "They're brought, bought and sold." Joe thought back to the face of the man he had tried to give water. His expression wasn't fearful, he remembered, but resigned. "After everything, this," it seemed to say. There was almost a quality of bemusement to it. Once the police had come and questioned them, Theresa hadn't been able to speak for hours. Joe had tried to wash the blood off of her, but it was persistent. It hadn't all come off until after she'd showered in the motel in Brawley, a pink trickle down the drain. Theresa hadn't been the same since. She had nightmares, real terrors. They were moving in together as soon as they could find a place, but Joe wasn't sure where the money was coming from. He had lost his classes at South Bay in the fall because their numbers were down. "Last hired, first fired," his friend Mike had said knowingly. "Business as usual." All he had left were two courses at Central. He hadn't had the heart to tell Theresa yet, not now. Maybe she could get him a job in the bookstore, Joe thought ruefully. He didn't know if he could stomach anything else.

Joe turned back around and watched a tall, blond woman jog toward him, her body toned and glistening with sweat in the sunshine. Who made her shoes, he wondered, imagining the scarred hands that stitched seams of her comfort. He turned back toward the water and spotted a few more sails drifting back and forth on the distant glow. For some reason, he thought of Nick Carraway in Fitzgerald's *The Great Gatsby* sitting by another coast, pondering the gorgeous dream of the orgiastic future, the boats, even then, rushing against the current. He had come west to this town south of Los Angeles, drifted in from Toledo driven by some vague notion of possibility, decades after the dream had lost its luster. He felt outside of it all, but that was a lie. There was no escaping the bonds of history, the headlong rush of time. It was what you did with your time that mattered. How you redeemed each moment that you occupied. Joe glanced to his side and noticed a young boy casting a fishing line into the harbor. A seagull flew overhead. He closed his eyes and thought about the migrants he'd seen die, the woman he loved, all the people he'd known, all those he hadn't, those who'd lived before him, those who would follow, everything, and all the joy and death and struggle. The breeze picked up and gently caressed his face, bringing him hints of faraway places. It was all part of the same thing, he thought. Somehow he would make it right.

a language that could speak to the dead

36

Theresa stood on her back porch staring at the hypnotic red pulse of the El Cortez sign, the downtown skyline beyond it. She watched a light go off in a distant highrise, heard the sound of a plane landing at Lindbergh field, and put her hand on her belly. There was no way she was two weeks late, she told herself. She must be pregnant. That was one thing she was good at. She hadn't told Joe yet, and she wondered how he'd feel about it. He and Mike were out playing pool tonight, but she hadn't been in the mood, that and Ceci. Tomorrow she and Joe were going to look at a place in City Heights. It should feel perfect, but it didn't. Theresa walked back in and peeked in at Cecilia in her bed, sleeping peacefully. She stared at her lying in the shadows for a long time.

Everything was all right, she told herself. Back out on the porch, Theresa leaned against the rail of the stairway and tried to imagine her future, but she couldn't. Every time she tried to let her mind wander, the woman's face came back to her, whispering plaintively, trying to say something that she couldn't understand. Theresa wiped her tears away and thought about what Mike had told her, that there were immigrants' rights groups, anti-slavery groups. It wasn't right, she thought. There must be something she could do. But in the cool darkness, it didn't help her—nothing seemed to be able to wipe it away.

Theresa was exhausted, but she was afraid to go to bed. She would fall asleep and then the dream would come, every time. Her legs seemed to resist her moving but eventually she went inside, locked the back door and walked into the bedroom. She slipped off her clothes, put on an oversized T-shirt, and got into bed. The Neruda book on her nightstand offered a brief respite. She read a poem without reading it, focusing on each word separately in a disconnected fashion. Then she read a full line: "Inside of me, the unwavering light." Theresa put the book down, but left the light on. Slowly, she drifted back into the desert where she held the woman in her arms. The woman was weeping and trying futilely to say something to her, but the words wouldn't come out. Finally, when they did, Theresa couldn't understand them. The old woman repeated something over and over again desperately, but she couldn't make it out. She shook her head apologetically but the woman's tears still turned red and flowed ever more steadily, until they became a river of blood that overflowed, flooding the desert and engulfing them, drowning everything in a sea of thick, red blood. Theresa woke up gasping for air, wishing for a way out of the dream, a language that could speak to the dead.